Red Light at Night
A Chase Gordon Tropical Thriller
Douglas Pratt

MANTA
PRESS

MANTA PRESS

For Ashlee

1

Carina's bow dipped as the keel cut through the crest of the wave. A southern wind swept in at about twelve knots on my beam. It had been blowing to my port for the last three and a half hours. My boom swung to starboard as the mainsail and the jib billowed with the steady air. There was enough of a chop to slow my speed as the hull of my Tartan forty-foot sailboat climbed up the five-to-six-foot seas before crashing down the other side.

Stretched out on the starboard bench, I stared off across the blue water. The evening sun was dropping over the edge of the ocean. No matter how many times I've seen the sunset, I'm drawn every night to it. The speed with which the bright yellow star softens to a smooth orange sphere as it descends into the sea always amazes me. Even the early morning sunrises, while swift in their dawning, seem slower than the end of the day. Perhaps it's because my attention remains locked on the radiant ball as it gives way to the encroaching twilight, but the descent is always perceptible.

Inevitably, it arrives faster than expected. One minute, the sun beams down from ten to fifteen degrees above the horizon. Still a yellow flame, it seems, at that point, that there will be plenty of daylight left. Suddenly, the gleams of bright light soften.

Most people think that the more brilliant sunsets come from clear, cloudless days. However, after basking in hundreds on the open water, I've learned something different. There is an exact number of clouds that create the perfect sunset. It needs to be enough to capture the red glow from the burning orb as it reaches through the last few degrees to the border. Too many clouds obscure the light. Not enough, and the glow diffuses across the sky.

Sailors for centuries estimated the weather from the last seconds of the day. The most famous of phrases taught to every new seaman was, "Red sky at night, sailor's delight." This forecasting guide dated back to biblical times and likely some shepherd or sailor coined it long before even that. Reddish hues spread across the sky, indicating the weather the next day would be clear. There were scientific reasonings that confounded me, but I knew it had to do with the dust particles and water vapor in the air. Whatever the technicalities behind the adage, it was a useful device for sailors traversing the seas in the days before satellite internet and Doppler technologies.

The evening's sky was already offering a fair forecast as the yellow sky burned a bright orange, only to shift to the gleaming red.

I pulled myself to my feet, feeling the motion of the deck under my bare soles. *Carina* edged through the waves that were shrinking as night crept up from behind me. Across the bow, I watched the half ball of red gleam almost brighter in those last few moments before the impending darkness snuffed out the orb. Intent on the line where the sea met sky, I searched for the peculiar phenomenon of the green flash. It's an optical illusion that can occur on the water when the last remnants of sunlight pass below the skyline. Occasionally, one can catch the flare of green light as the atmosphere acts as a prism for the yellow solar light.

Tonight, the flash eluded me. It wasn't uncommon, but they were still hard to glimpse. The conditions tonight offered the chance.

However, on the horizon, a new light caught my attention. Another boat steamed through the southern waters of the Gulf of Mexico. I hadn't noticed the shape in the distance, but now that the light escaped around the hemisphere, I made out the bright lights glowing off the decks. It was about two miles out and moving at what I estimated to be fifteen to twenty knots.

As the surrounding sea grew dark on the moonless evening, I realized I hadn't illuminated my running lights. It was an irritatingly common mistake on my part. I'd get so wrapped up in the pomp and circumstance I mentally created around the sunset that I'd forget to flip the switch.

Both hands grasped either side of the open companionway, and I swung through the opening, landing with both feet on the sole below. The heel of the Tartan was more prominent in the cabin, and I leaned to port. *Carina* coursed along at about ten degrees to port. Enough to notice the tilt without sending everything scattering across the cabin.

With a flick of my wrist, I threw the breaker that operated the running lights. At the same time, I turned on the deck lights, two LED spotlights attached to the spreaders halfway up the mast. The two bulbs bathed the cockpit and foredeck with white light. When I was near the coast, the lights brought in every mosquito, moth, and mayfly from a hundred-mile radius to swarm *Carina*. But a hundred miles from dry ground, there was rarely anything flying around out here. I could enjoy the night air without fear of being devoured.

I opened the little refrigerator in my galley and removed a bottle of water. Recently, I picked up several reusable water bottles that I could easily refill from larger containers and slip into the fridge. With three extras, I rotated one in to chill with everyone I took out. It kept me hydrated with cold water—a luxury at sea—without creating needless trash. Space on a forty-foot sailboat remained limited. Not to mention, the number of bottles I saw floating over thirty miles from shore disturbed me. I didn't want to add to the problem any more than I needed to.

Next to the water bottle was the last of the turkey I'd bought in Key West. It took me just a minute to throw together a turkey sandwich. Since I had no more lettuce or tomatoes, it only consisted of meat, mayonnaise, and the last two pieces of bread, one of which was the heel. Still, the sandwich hit the spot, and I was two bites into it when I came back on deck.

The other vessel had closed the distance toward me. It was moving at least twice as fast as I was, but then I was in no hurry. In another hour, I'd pull in the jib and let the mainsail push me through the night. It would slow my progress, but I'd catch a few hours of sleep in the cockpit. The radar and AIS would alert me if anything came close. Besides, I'd long learned the art of sleeping lightly. In the Corps, sleep came whenever I could fit it in. If I was in the field, that might mean a nap while standing against a wall.

The AIS, or Automatic Identification System, was a transmitter and receiver that could detect other vessels in the vicinity. Any ships on the screen appeared with their location relative to *Carina*'s and a vessel name, although sometimes shortened. The AIS shortened the name this time, listing it as "SER ODSY."

My eyes squinted as I made out the lines of the approaching yacht. It was large, measuring well over fifty feet. Probably over seventy-five. I didn't recognize the make or model, but that meant next to nothing. There were so many yachts on the water that it was difficult to remember every make. This one looked to be on the higher end of the spectrum, making it less likely I'd run across one too often.

I reached over to the radio, lifting the receiver. When there were only two of you on an expanse of open water, it might be impolite not to at least offer a greeting.

"Motor yacht, this is SV *Carina*," I called through the radio.

"*Carina*, this is MV *Serendipity's Odyssey*. Where are you out of?" The voice on the air was gruff and male.

"Sailed out of Key West two days ago. Heading toward Isla Mujeres."

"Roger, Captain. We passed Mujeres leaving Cozumel."

"Roger," I acknowledged. "Seas seem to be calming down. Not that you can feel them, right?"

"It might shock you how much the flybridge sways," the other captain remarked. "I'll take less chop."

I grinned. "You got a nice ride," I told him.

"You too," he replied. "Nothing quite as pretty as sails filled with air."

"I'd have to agree with you," I admitted. "How was the traffic where you came from?"

"You're the first company I've seen in the last eight hours."

"Good to know," I replied. "You should be clear for a few hundred miles. It's been quiet since I skirted Cuba."

I turned as the yacht passed on the port beam about a mile south of me. I couldn't make out any figures from this distance, only the lights of the cabin glowing against the black sea. The drone of its engine reverberated across the water. Had my diesel been churning, I might not have noticed the noise, but with only the wind driving me forward, the mechanical whirring sounded foreign out here.

With the microphone still in my grip, my eyes shifted back to the receiver. We'd passed the cordiality test, and there was little we were going to converse about over the radio waves.

"Fair winds," I offered as a farewell.

"Same to you, Captain. Perhaps we'll see you in port some—" The sentence never ended as a crackle of static burst through the speakers a millisecond before the *whoomph* sounded. I turned my head to see the flybridge of the yacht explode in a plume of red-orange fire. Even a mile away, instinct caused me to raise my forearm to shield myself from debris that would never come this far. I heard the second explosion, having covered my face for a split second. My hand jerked down as the aft deck exploded in a third fireball that sent fiberglass and wood shrapnel in every direction. The giant vessel was barely visible through the towering flames leaping from the decks.

I spun the wheel, forgetting to disengage my autopilot. As soon as *Carina* made a complete turn, the autopilot attempted to engage and turn her back in the direction I'd originally been heading. My fingers slipped below the wheel to disengage the gear that connected the autopilot to the helm. The wheel loosened as the gears no longer attempted to turn.

The jib luffed as the bow turned through the wind. I was slow to react, and when I'd made an about-face, the wind filled the foresail from the opposite side. I scrambled to release the sheet, securing it to the starboard winch. The line whistled as it whipped through the blocks. The jib filled with wind, and I barely got my hands on the line to pull it in before *Carina* heeled to port at a stark angle. In a few seconds, I tightened the sail and trimmed it down. *Carina* righted herself to a more reasonable angle as she cut through the water toward the ball of fire.

I grabbed the radio to call out a mayday. There was no response. We were too far from anyone to receive the call. Ahead, flames danced across the water, casting a red glow against the black sky.

2

Flames seemed to emerge from the ocean, and the orange glow reflected off the dark water. The diesel engine rumbled beneath me as I guided *Carina* toward the wreckage. Once I turned the Tartan toward the burning remnants of *Serendipity's Odyssey*, I started the motor. I wanted more control at the helm when I reached the explosion site. With the propeller driving *Carina* forward now, I furled the jib sail, pulling on the Dacron line connected to the drum at the bottom of the sail. The drum emitted a high-pitched squeal as it turned, rolling the canvas up along the foil. The clew flapped in the wind as the sail released the air and recoiled. In seconds, I heard the telltale flap of the line slapping against the tightly wrapped jib.

With a flick of the cam cleat securing the mainsail's halyard, the line whipped through the hole as gravity took hold, and the sail dropped onto the boom. The lazy jack system I installed on *Carina* allowed the sail to come down somewhat neatly as it descended. Without it, the canvas would fold in a heap across the cockpit, held aloft only by the boom, and I would need to flake it and secure it to keep it out of the way.

Now that both sails were down, the boat operated solely under power. My hands turned the wheel, steering the sailboat around the burning wreckage. I pulled the throttle back to neutral, staying about sixty feet away from the nearest flame. Scrambling on top of the cabin, I scanned the surface for survivors. Other than the flickering flames rising and sinking with the waves, the sea appeared lifeless. Even the fires were burning down, likely having devoured most of the diesel fuel spread over the sea.

I jumped back down into the cockpit, opened the lazarette on the starboard side, and removed a spotlight. The 90,000-lumen light came on in my hands as I crawled toward the bow. The beam illuminated the water, spreading the white light over the ocean.

I sucked in a breath as I surveyed the debris of the yacht. Nothing remained but some flotsam that would stay on the surface. The hull had already gone under, swallowed by the waters of the Gulf. By now, it had either settled on the ocean floor, about six thousand feet below me, or was on a rapid descent there.

The glow of light stretched over the water, reflecting off the oily seawater. No one seemed to be in the water.

I considered lowering my dinghy to search closer to the wreckage, but in the dark, it might prove more dangerous. If I struck something a few feet under the surface, I risked puncturing the inflatable material. For a brief second, I missed *Beth*, my old wooden dinghy.

After returning to the cockpit, I slipped the throttle into a low gear. *Carina* inched forward, pitching in the chop. My left hand held the spotlight, shining it out into the darkness, as I veered around the perimeter of the debris field.

Cushions, singed from the fire, floated, and I strained to search for anyone holding on to them. Light splayed across what might have been a table or a wooden countertop. The wood bobbed unnaturally. I focused the beam on it again, shrinking the aperture on the lens to a thin laser-like point; the object was definitely a table. I recognized the slats of teak. It had probably been on one of the upper decks when the boat exploded. The piece of furniture would float for days, if not weeks.

The table moved again, nudged from somewhere beneath the surface. I turned to port, taking *Carina* on a direct heading for the object. The danger of moving too close was the same thing I feared in the dinghy. The wreckage might still be buoyant enough to float just under the surface. An impact on the Tartan's fiberglass hull could tear a gash on the bottom and break the number one rule of sailing—keep the ocean outside the boat.

At near idle, the danger diminished but had not been eliminated. A collision would still damage the hull, but with such slow momentum, I hoped it would be nothing more than a thump, resulting in minimal damage. I climbed onto the port bench, keeping one hand within grasp of the helm and the other shining the light on the water.

The piece of furniture dropped under like a fishing bobber. I couldn't see beneath the surface. The light reflected. The table rotated forty-five degrees before being pulled under the water again.

I resisted the urge to dive in. Logic pointed out I'd seen no sign of a survivor, and the movement could have resulted from anything. Without knowing what might be under the surface, I didn't want to chance tangling myself in something I couldn't see.

The table surfaced again, popping up out of the water like a cork. I reached back and steered the boat closer. When I was within ten feet, I retrieved the boat hook hanging off the starboard railing. The hook extended to eight feet, and I pulled it out to its entire length. Stretching over the side, I let the metal finger at the end come down on the wooden surface with a thud. I leaned over the side of the cockpit as I tried to reach another three inches to the opposite side. The crook wrapped around the edge, and I pulled it toward me.

Something pulled at it, and I felt resistance as it tried to drag away from me. My arm jerked inward against it, and the flotsam bumped against *Carina*'s hull. Hanging my torso over the side, I reached down to pull the table out of the water.

The white mass lunged out of the dark, and I pulled back as the wide head crashed down on the tabletop, shoving it beneath the surface. The gray dorsal fin submerged a millisecond later, and I stared at the black water.

It took another five seconds before the fin broke
through again as it circled back to the table. The tiger shark
passed only a few feet from me. At that moment, I decided
reaching back into the water for the table wasn't an option.
Instead, I grabbed the light and shone it down, widening
the aperture to spread the light over the surface.

Just below the water, I could see a pinkish thing floating
under the table. In fact, it appeared to be attached to it. Or
rather, the table snagged it.

It's a fucking hand.

Really, it was only part of a hand and a forearm. I stared
at it for a second, debating to myself how workable it was
to grab it. A flash of gray thrashed through the water, and
the wooden table submerged in a rush. The brown mass
retreated underwater. The sound of wood scraping along
the hull indicated it was dragging across the bottom of
Carina. I cringed at the thought of the wood marring up
the bottom side.

Stupid thought, Gordon. That's a person.

I jumped to the starboard bench and shone the light
across the water. There was no sign of the table, the hand,
or the shark. He must have been worried I was about
to take the rest of his meal, and rather than lose his last
morsel, he took off with it.

A burp of water sounded about fifty feet off the
starboard bow, and I scanned the surface. The table floated
on the surface again. There was little chance there was
much left of the hand now. Instead, I turned my attention
back to the remnants of *Serendipity's Odyssey*.

The throttle slipped into idle again, and I circled the sea-drift. Again, I tried the radio, calling for anyone out there. Still no response. I would need to go below and use the single-side band or SSB to call farther than the VHF would handle. The SSB, similar to a HAM radio, could bounce its signal much farther than the line of sight that the VHF offered. However, before I climbed below, I wanted to move away from the debris field. If something fouled the prop now, it would stay fouled. Hell couldn't get me in the water with a feeding tiger shark.

Before I got too far, I wanted to give the radius another pass. I doubted there were any survivors, but I didn't want to find out I'd missed one. As I rounded the flotsam, I spotted the dorsal fin shadowing me. The surreal scene left me uneasy as the adrenaline coursing through my body had receded. How many people were on the boat? Who were these people I'd just witnessed die?

I motored about fifty yards south, where I cut the wheel to starboard and pulled the throttle back to neutral. The sea had calmed since the sun set, and now there was only a gentle rocking as *Carina* wound in circles.

In the cabin, I called the Coast Guard Station in New Orleans. It was a toss-up whether New Orleans or Miami was closer. Technically, both Cuba and Mexico were closer, but that created red tape I didn't want to finagle.

Once I connected, I gave Ensign Maryweather the details of the incident, including the time of the explosion and the coordinates.

"Are there any survivors?" he asked.

"I've searched. All hands went down with the vessel," I responded, realizing the unfortunate pun I'd just made. Even my often-macabre sense of humor spurned the turn of phrase.

"We have a cutter that will be there in a few hours. Are you able to remain in the vicinity?"

"Yes," I assured the ensign. I didn't intend on leaving, anyway. Whoever died tonight left me as a witness, and until I passed that baton off to someone else, I would stand guard over their grave.

When I signed off with the ensign, I returned to the helm, steering *Carina* back toward the wreckage. There would be no sleep tonight.

3

The island displayed only a little green from offshore. In fact, it didn't seem to rise much out of the sea. Based on the charts, Isla Mujeres had an altitude of only one meter above sea level. Not much more than an atoll, Isla Mujeres was less than twenty kilometers from mainland Mexico. However, Bahia Mujeres separated the mainland from the island. A ferry traveled back and forth across the bay, but it limited the throngs of tourists, eliminating the all-inclusive crowds in Cancun that only wanted to visit Mexico in name only.

I'd never been here, and when I first planned the crossing from Key West, I read up on the city. The warm waters surrounding it invited dolphins, turtles, rays, and, for me, sharks. Just off the eastern shoreline was a diving location called *La Cueva de los Tiburones Dormidos*, or the Cave of the Sleeping Sharks. Between this unusual diving spot and the *Museo Subaquático de Arte,* an underwater art exhibit designed to highlight the effects of climate change, I expected to find a unique destination for scuba diving.

At the outset of my trip, I'd planned to be anchored near the *La Cueva de los Tiburones Dormidos* tonight so that I

could get in an early dive tomorrow. But the explosion of
Serendipity's Odyssey derailed that plan. I remained near
the coordinates of the wreckage for four hours before
the USCGC *Divisive* arrived on scene. After that, it was
another three hours of questions and interrogation. By the
time they gave me permission to leave, the morning sun
was coming up.

I sailed about twenty-five miles west before I dropped
the sails and turned the wheel all the way to starboard.
With the engine off, any forward movement came from
the wind and current, but with the rudder spun to the
side, the Tartan made a tight circle. I stretched out on
the cockpit bench and closed my eyes. The AIS and radar
guaranteed that if any other vessels approached, the alarms
would rouse me long before they came near.

After three hours, I sat up. Some subconscious dream
startled me awake, but now, in the daylight, I didn't recall
what it was. Those few hours sustained me for the next
twenty as I continued on toward Isla Mujeres. The current
only carried me about two miles off course during that
time, and I hoisted the sails to speed along.

But the delay was enough to change my plans. Besides
some quick catnaps, I hadn't slept since then because as
I neared Mexico, boat traffic increased, and I didn't trust
some fool in a cigarette boat not to run up on me at ninety
miles per hour.

I would need to check into Mexico with the customs
officials anyway, so I headed around to the western side
of the island. Before I left the Keys, a cruiser who'd spent
some time here recommended El Milagro Marina, and

when I approached it, I found a single dock jutting out from shore with nine yachts tied up alongside.

The dockmaster, who spoke only a little more English than I did Spanish, directed me, after some difficulty, to pull up next to a fifty-two-foot Fountaine Pajot catamaran. As *Carina* inched up along the wooden pier, a gaunt kid in his teens came running out to catch my dock lines. He secured the bow and stern lines to separate cleats. When I disembarked, I gave the boy three dollars. I didn't like tipping in US currency when I was cruising, but I only had about a hundred pesos on board. That would have wiped me out, and I needed to find a bank before I headed to the immigration office.

I'd raised the white quarantine flag on *Carina*'s stern. Once I'd cleared immigration, I could hoist the Mexican flag I had on hand. The process was the same in every country, and it seemed somewhat foolish to me. Yet, I'd prefer not to have some deranged immigration officer toss me in jail and attempt to confiscate my home.

"Taxi?" I asked the kid.

"They can call you one at the office," he replied in perfect English.

"Thanks." I felt the exhaustion creeping up on me. I needed to stay up at least until the late afternoon. If I crashed now, I'd end up waking up in about eight or nine hours as the sun was going down again. It would throw my entire sleep schedule off. Besides, I wanted to clear in to Mexico and find some food. If I was lucky, there might be a hot shower somewhere around here.

Every time I hit solid land after several days on the boat,
I get an unusual sensation. I'm sure there's a term for
it in the sailing community, but I just refer to it as "the
wobbles." My legs shake, and I feel like I'm tilting from
side to side. As soon as I stepped off the pier, the feeling
struck me. I grabbed a bench to steady myself. A pale
man stared at me from a wrought-iron patio table about a
hundred feet away. The man was in his forties and looked
like some typical American tourist with a pale tan linen
jacket and pants over a sky-blue buttoned-down shirt. He
wore a small fedora that matched his suit.

At least he didn't go for the traditional Panama hat.

He seemed intent on me, but he didn't move.
Such attention wasn't uncommon after arriving in a
marina. Fellow cruisers and liveaboards grew curious
about the newcomer, until someone came around to
ask the important questions—like "Where have you
come from?" which was followed often by "Oh, do you
know so-and-so?" The cruising community was small and
tight-knit. If there was ever a place to play the game of Six
Degrees of Separation, the local marinas were it.

He didn't acknowledge me, and I, likewise, ignored him
as I strolled past. There'd be a time to chat him up if he was
on one of the other boats.

I entered the office to see a young girl about the same age
as the dock hand.

"Are you on the *Carina*?" she asked in English. Her face
resembled that of the boy, and it was a fair bet they were
siblings. The youth were being raised up to speak English,
and they seemed to run the docks already because of that.

"Yes, I just docked. I need to head down to the immigration office."

The girl gave me a nod and lifted the phone, dialing a number. She said something in Spanish and hung up. "There's a car coming out front. When you get back, I'll get you taken care of."

Mexico, like most Caribbean nations I'd visited, kept the immigration process easy. Within fifteen minutes of entering, the official had permitted me to stay for up to six months. Once my time was done, I could check out from any immigration office. The driver who brought me here was still waiting out front in his Volkswagen Jetta.

I paused when I spotted the same man I'd seen coming off the dock. He was getting out of a car down the street. Without turning my attention to him, I scanned the streets. There were several businesses along the divided brick-lined street, including an Oxxo corner store, at least two banks, and many shops and restaurants. After all, the island was tiny, only about five miles from the northern tip to the southern.

Still, Fedora stared at me as I got back into the vehicle. As the driver pulled off the curb, I turned around in the back seat to watch the man who was no longer beside the car.

You're getting paranoid, Gordon.

Not that it was hard to get to that point. After all, I was running on almost no sleep, and witnessing the explosion on the yacht and subsequent deaths of its occupants still weighed on my mind. I'd spent the four hours waiting for the Coast Guard mulling over what I'd seen. There were three distinct explosions. Although it was feasible that the yacht had two fuel tanks. Once one explodes, the second might follow just like it had. But what would cause the first fireball?

I'm a logical individual, and one thing I hate is coincidence. In three days at sea, I'd only passed one other boat once I was away from land. And that vessel blew up and sunk right before my eyes. It didn't seem statistically possible.

That didn't mean it wasn't. After all, such wild things happen, and I somehow seem to attract those incidents.

But there were questions I didn't like. This new variable added to my unease.

As I mused about things I couldn't control, my stomach grumbled, and I realized I hadn't eaten since mid-afternoon yesterday.

"Can you drop me over there?" I asked the driver, pointing at a blue building with a red door and window frames. The words "*La Casa Azul*" stretched over the window in hand-painted lettering. Another sign read "*Rinconcito Kahlo.*" The Jetta slid to a stop, and I climbed out, passing the driver a hundred pesos. I sighed with relief, grateful that I'd found a bank next to the immigration office. Now I was flush with pesos.

Inside the little cafe, I found several small white tables and folding chairs. A large painting of Frida Kahlo adorned one wall. The other side of the small restaurant held a counter with the same matching white tiles that covered the floor. A woman with a long black ponytail lifted her head from a tray of dough balls on parchment paper.

The woman glanced up at me. Her face contorted as she wiped flour-coated palms on the black apron covering a red t-shirt. "*Hola, siéntate,*" she greeted me, waving her still-white hand at the empty tables.

My grasp of Spanish was minimal, and despite attempting to increase my knowledge, I only understood the "*hola*" in her sentence. Using context clues, I assumed she was telling me to take a seat. I pulled out a chair and settled at a small four-top table.

She came around the bar and handed me a paper menu. I scanned the page that was in Spanish.

"*Birria tacos, por favor,*" I requested "And that Jamaica Miel Loco." I pointed at one of the colorful bottles in a row of beers.

The woman nodded, as if she knew I'd strained myself to get that much Spanish out. She returned less than a minute later with an opened long neck of beer. The label read "Isla Brewing Company." I turned up the bottle and swallowed a gulp.

I hadn't had a drink since I left Florida. Not that I required one. It wasn't something I craved by any means. My self-imposed rules prevent me from drinking too much anyway, and I never consume alcohol when I'm at sea. While I trusted myself in most situations, I also knew that in a pinch, it was better to remain clearheaded.

The notion brought my thoughts back to *Serendipity's Odyssey*. Suddenly, the beer acted more like a salve than anything else. It lost some flavor as I recalled I was mid-sentence with the captain when the yacht exploded.

The aroma of roasted meat filled the room, and I saw the woman come back toward me carrying a ceramic plate with three birria tacos.

"*Gracias.*"

Again, she only nodded before returning to the dough balls that ultimately would turn into fresh tortillas. I lifted the taco and took a bite. The grease from the meat dribbled out the back of the taco, and I instinctively pulled back to prevent the liquid from splattering my shirt. Not that it was special, just a rash guard I used to protect my arms from the sun.

As I chewed, the seat across from me pulled back and the man in the linen suit sat down across from me. He removed the fedora and set it down on the table next to him. My eyes lifted to look at the man.

"Mind if I join you?" he asked in a sardonic tone.

4

I stared at the man across from me. He was about my age, although I guessed he had me by a few years. The first thing I noticed was the long, crooked nose that hooked down like a raptor's beak. Pale cheekbones indicated he didn't spend too much time in the sun, or he had one of those complexions that never absorbed the ultraviolet rays. He couldn't be called gaunt, but his face was sallow. In his other hand, he swung a pair of Ray-Ban sunglasses that Tom Cruise could have worn. My eyes locked with his.

"Did I do something to indicate to you that I wanted company?" I questioned, still holding the last bite of my birria taco. Grease dripped off the morsel, pooling on my paper plate.

The pale bird man shrugged. "I thought you might want to talk."

Without saying a word, I popped the last chunk of meat and tortilla shell into my mouth. Each movement of my jaw was deliberate and slow until, after twenty seconds, I swallowed.

"I don't," I assured him, taking a swallow of the jamaica-flavored beer.

He cocked his head, reading the label. "Jamaica?" he questioned, pronouncing the word like the island country. "What is it?"

"Jamaica," I corrected, enunciating the guttural fricative of the traditional H in English. "It's a flower. Like a hibiscus."

Birdman pursed his lips, nodding as if intrigued by the idea. He motioned to the woman behind the bar. "*¿Puedo tener una cerveza también?*"

His Spanish sounded flawless, and I realized he was toying with me. A few seconds later, the woman pressing out tortillas crossed the room to set a bottle in front of him.

I took another pull on the bottle.

"You don't want to ask who I am?" he wondered.

My head shook.

"The name's Andrew Smith," he introduced himself, sticking his right hand out to me.

"Smith?" I questioned, ignoring the outstretched palm.

He retracted it and lifted the beer to his lips. "You don't like my name?"

"Kinda generic," I remarked.

"That's harsh," he countered.

"It would be," I agreed, "if it were your real name."

He didn't respond.

"What do you want?" I asked him.

"To talk to you," he told me. "Like I said, I'm Andrew Smith."

"You're a spook," I stated.

He gave me a half smile. "What makes you say that?"

"I've worked with my fair share of CIA agents. You fit the bill."

"That's profiling," he pointed out.

"That only matters if it negatively affects you."

"Chase, do you mind if I call you 'Chase'?"

"Smith, there's nothing to talk about. My last run-in with the Agency left me in a bind."

"Technically, that wasn't the CIA," he reminded me while pointing out he knew my history. "In fact, I believe the Agency helped get you out of that mess."

I took another drink before cocking my head and answering, "I'm pretty sure the president had more to do with that."

"Look, Gordon, we can volley this back and forth all day. In the end, I think you'll help me."

"Do what?" I questioned.

"First, I want to talk to you about what happened the other night."

There it was. I assumed Smith sat with me for that reason.

"I don't know shit about that. Although, I assume if you are here, then you read whatever report the Coast Guard wrote up. In that case, you know everything I told them."

"Come now, Gordon, you are too keen to fool me," he retorted as he leaned back in his chair. "A guy like you witnesses something like that. What are the odds?"

"What are you saying?" I demanded.

"I don't like coincidences," Smith explained. "How does the same guy who got mixed up in Cuba with the president's son happen across an accident at sea?"

I shrugged. "Don't ask me," I said. What I didn't do was agree with him. I didn't like the coincidence either. But I'd already questioned that myself. Besides, I felt an instant dislike to this man, who may have been implying I had something to do with the explosion.

"It just leaves questions," he remarked. "You don't seem too shaken up by the whole thing. Here you are just two days later enjoying all Isla Mujeres has to offer. Cold beer, tacos."

My arms folded across my chest, and I tilted my head, studying the man. He wanted to get under my skin. I guessed he thought he could manipulate me into something with veiled accusations and suppositions.

"Listen, Smith, I know what kind of game you are trying to play. I've been in some intense situations where men I knew and cared for died. If you think watching men die on a boat a mile away doesn't linger with me, then you're an idiot."

Smith stared back at me.

"I've been hip-deep in death before, and every time it sticks with me. But I can't let it push me down."

"But you don't want to do anything about it?" he queried.

"I did," I refuted. "I attempted a rescue at sea. Unfortunately, there was nothing to save."

"You can dig around in it," he suggested.

"Nope," I answered. "I don't have any desire."

"Look, we need someone to find out what happened to that yacht," he told me.

"Ah, there's the hook," I noted. "I'm not interested."

"This isn't like something you do for free," he explained. "The Agency would pay you."

"Still not interested," I repeated, pushing away from the table. "I'm planning to enjoy the island and all Isla Mujeres offers."

"Gordon, wait," he pleaded.

"Smith, you interrupted my first taco," I informed him, sliding the two other tacos across the table to him. "Enjoy the rest of them. I'll assume you are going to pay the tab."

I walked past the giant wall mural of Frida Kahlo, leaving Smith in the little restaurant. As I came out of the open door, my hand shielded my eyes. My driver had gone on to his next fare or whatever he was doing. I walked back rather than wait for a taxi.

After crossing the street, I headed north on the sidewalk. To my right and past the white barricade along the road was a wall of trees. I glanced back to see Smith standing outside the restaurant, watching me. It seemed odd that he'd gotten here so soon after the tragedy.

If his goal had been to poke the curiosity in me, he'd done a good job. Already, my mind filled with questions.

Now, I wondered what, or, rather, who, would be so important to get the CIA involved. Not just that, but Smith wasn't waiting around on the island for me.

Or was he?

I had a flashback to another CIA agent who sucked me into a job in Havana. Only the CIA hadn't sanctioned the job either. It had been a scam aimed at manipulating me.

Was this the same thing?

I wasn't sure, but I didn't care. Tomorrow, I planned to dive *La Cueva de los Tiburones Dormidos*. After that, I'd spend some time on the island doing exactly what Smith suggested. Until then, though, I planned to rest from the long transit.

5

The sea remained calm as I skimmed over the tops of the waves. The early morning sun gleamed off the water, and I had to drop the handheld chartplotter below the inflatable tubes in order to see the screen. I veered to starboard to follow the suggested course.

La Cueva de los Tiburones Dormidos lay about a mile off the northeastern tip of Isla Mujeres. A local fisherman discovered the cave in 1969 when he was free-diving for lobsters in the cavernous areas. Instead of the crustaceans, the man came across several bull and tiger sharks lying at the bottom of the cave. The discovery soon prompted explorers like Jacques Cousteau to come to see the cave. In fact, Cousteau claimed the discovery for himself, and it wasn't for a few years that the fisherman received the credit he was due.

Since the site was a little off the beaten path, it didn't get as many visitors as some of the more popular dive locations around Cancun. However, it still proved popular with the dive shops on the island. I'd checked with the local guides to find most didn't leave the docks until at least eight in the morning. My watch told me it was just a few minutes past seven. I should have a couple hours of dive time before the first boats arrived.

Guiding the tiller to starboard, I aimed the bow to the east. A dorsal fin came up about thirty feet off my port side. After the run-in with the tiger shark, I took an instant to look again as a second fin came out of the water. The two dolphins seemed to want to outrun me, and I wasn't about to race them. Instead, I kept the speed steady, allowing them to pace me.

Moments like this remind me why I love the sea. I traveled three days across the Gulf of Mexico without spotting a single dolphin—despite searching. I always monitored the water for any sign of them. When I first took *Carina* out, I spent two days scanning for any sign of dolphins. Often, I'd get excited at the sight of what I thought was a dorsal fin, only to find it was a wave. Now that I'd been living full time on the water, I realized that when a dolphin showed up, which was often, it was obvious I was seeing an animal and not an optical illusion.

I wondered if the pair would follow me to the cave. They might scare away any sharks that might be there, but it was hard not to be excited to have the company.

Unfortunately, my two new traveling companions soon grew bored with the droning outboard and changed their heading to the north. I followed them with my eyes as they continued the rhythmic porpoising. Eventually, they either dove beneath the waters or got far enough out of my sight.

I steered the inflatable on for another ten minutes before the chartplotter indicated I was almost on top of the site. My dinghy didn't come with a depth gauge, but I'd researched the area, finding it to be about sixty to sixty-five feet deep.

After releasing the throttle, I moved forward to the bow where I lowered a twenty-two-pound anchor hand over hand. I didn't want to drop the thing on a sleeping shark. The line slipped through my grip, and I'd slow it down if it slid too fast. The anchor was far heavier than I needed for the rigid inflatable boat, but I'd found it on a dive after some poor slob's rode broke. Free anchors are a gift from the sea that should never be turned down.

Once the hook settled on the ocean floor, I secured the line to the bow and returned aft to shut off the outboard. The inflatable bobbed in the waves, and I put my scuba gear together. I had two full Nitrox cylinders, but I doubted I'd end up using both. The dive should take me down to about sixty-five feet, which would give me around an hour. Each of the air tanks had about three thousand pounds of pressure, and I could dive almost two hours with that much air. But I like to be prepared, and the extra tank was just in case.

I slipped the Mares BCD, or buoyancy compensator device, onto the tank and tightened the strap. After attaching the first stage regulator to the cylinder valve, I checked the air levels in my cylinder. The needle sat just under the three thousand mark.

I expected the water temperature to be around eighty degrees, so I opted to only wear my Sharkskin wetsuit, a lighter one that gave me more freedom of movement. Once I slipped my fins onto my booted feet, I slid into

the BCD and pulled the mask over my head. I splashed
backwards off the starboard tube and righted myself in the
water.

Once I ensured that I was comfortable with how my
gear fit on me, I let the air out of my BCD and descended
toward the bottom. With the anchor rode as my guide,
I sank. The gush of bubbles as I exhaled echoed in my
ears. Most people who have never dived think that the
silence underwater must be nice, but that was a common
misconception. There was always the sound of bubbles,
and since it's inadvisable to stop breathing underwater,
they never stop. Still, I found the rhythmic gurgle relaxing.
It beat yoga.

At about twelve feet down, I cleared my ears as the water
pressure increased. That first time, I could often relieve
the pressure by flexing my jaw muscle. At twenty feet, the
sensation returned, and I had to pinch my nose to blow
gently. I heard the pressure pop, although I suspected it
wasn't something I could hear as much as feel.

My feet extended out behind me as I drifted
down. Below me, dark rocks grew closer. I checked
my depth—thirty-five feet. My arms swung clockwise,
rotating me around until I could see the surface retreating
from me.

Visibility extended at least sixty feet since I could see the
ocean floor. As I exhaled, I watched the rising bubbles,
counting the seconds until they reached the surface. With
a twist, I twirled back around to face the ocean floor.

My Mares dive computer strapped to my wrist told me
I was passing fifty feet. Several fish were coursing along

the bottom. One or two swam closer to inspect me, but as soon as I turned to get a closer look, they darted away.

Beneath me, a rocky mass grew closer, and I leveled out over the formation. A small school of bicolor damselfish weaved through the crevices and holes in the rock face. The brown and white fish nibbled on the rocks, feeding on the plankton and microscopic life.

Kicking twice, my fins propelled me along the edge of the rock. The descent continued down around the formation, and I followed the face toward the sandy bottom. A surgeonfish meandered over the rocks. Its blue-green lateral fins seemed to glow in the filtered sunlight from above. It paid me little attention; instead it glided away from me.

I settled about a foot off the sand, just floating. Several more colorful varietals of small fish careened over the ocean floor. I kicked twice, sending me along the sand. The mounds of rock loomed above me, casting shadows. My dive computer confirmed I was at sixty-two feet and the water temperature was a comfortable eighty degrees, especially in the Sharkskin.

Before I swam off, I found the anchor and took a bearing off my compass. To the north, another rock formation sat, and I suspected it was the entrance to the cave. There was no rush, so I soaked in the surroundings.

The entrance to the cave only gave me about four feet of clearance. Before entering, I retrieved the dive light I kept clipped to the side of my BCD. The beam illuminated the inside of the cave.

I'd been anticipating this dive with some excitement. Despite the run-in with the tiger shark the other night, I found the creatures fascinating. That doesn't sound like much considering I get excited about most undersea life, but sharks carry such intrigue and excitement with them. After all, I always sided with the shark in *Jaws*. She was just hungry. Besides, they weren't as frightening as the movies made them out. Hundreds of thousands of people swim with sharks every year, and there are only a handful of incidents. There's more danger driving down I-95 to Miami.

La Cueva de los Tiburones Dormidos offered a unique opportunity. Sharks are notorious for their inability to remain motionless. Most species require constant movement to allow the flow of water through their gills, so it is rare to find them motionless. Somehow, in this cave, though, they can rest on the bottom of the sea. Scientists surmised it might be the perfect storm, where the current and temperature allowed the shark a chance to relax, if that was what the creatures were doing.

Light splayed over the rocks as I inched into the crevasse. Inside the cavern, I felt cramped, and I worried the tank would bang on the ceiling. Bubbles streamed past my ears, collecting overhead as they wiggled their way behind me to the opening.

On the sand ahead of me, a four-foot bull shark stretched. His snub nose stared at me. I stroked my fin to send me to the right, so I wasn't staring face-to-face with the creature. As small as he was, he wouldn't be a threat unless he wanted to get out of the cavern and I was blocking his only exit. Even a little guy like him could tear me up in that confined space.

But the animal didn't move. I scanned along the gray skin. The shark's claspers were just visible as they jutted out from beneath the creature's belly. He was a male. The eyes stared ahead without blinking, and I drifted around him. If I'd wanted, I could reach out and run my hand over his skin. There was no point. If he was asleep, I might disturb him, and I'd touched enough sharks in my time. There's a misconception that animals want to be petted. Most probably don't, and they will inform the person petting them if they don't like it. I'd just as soon keep my fingers.

The warm current swirled around me, carrying me in a sweeping motion around the shark. As I passed his caudal fin, I saw another larger shark deeper in the cave. My hand pushed me off the sand as I gave a soft kick that propelled me deeper into the cave. My flashlight illuminated the cavernous opening that expanded as I entered it.

Inside, the sole occupant was another bull shark, a thirteen-footer. The beam streaked across its body, and I couldn't see any sex organs, which might mean it was female or that the male's claspers were tucked beneath him. Like its smaller brother, this one's eyes stared ahead. I kept the light away from its eyes. Instead, I trailed it along the beast's sleek silver body.

For what seemed like a brief moment, I floated in the cave of the sleeping sharks as motionless as the animals themselves. After minutes, I realized I'd fallen into a trance. The gentle, warm current combined with the low

light and steady gurgle of bubbles from my regulator lulled
me. For a time, I enjoyed the mindless peace of being a
shark.

The sudden beeping of my Mares dive computer
startled me, and I turned off the alarm that warned my
bottom time was about to expire. I took another long look
at the thirteen-foot behemoth. It was like sitting down to
meditate with a tiger.

I maneuvered back through the cave past the little bull
shark and kicked gently toward the mouth of the cave.
As I squeezed out the opening, I checked my computer.
The air tank still had twelve hundred pounds of air, but I
would need to be back in a no decompression depth soon.
I marked the direction with my compass before heading
toward the anchor. Since I knew the correct direction, I
angled my swim up so that I could take my time getting to
a shallower depth.

When I reached the anchor rode, I caught it with
my right hand. My depth was now at thirty-three feet.
Without inflating my BCD, I kicked twice, pushing my
body toward the surface. At fifteen feet, I leveled off,
adding a small amount of air to my vest to hold me neutral
while I waited five minutes at my safety stop.

When my head broke through the surface, the dinghy
floated beside me. Before slipping my arms out of the
BCD, I inflated it. Once out, I climbed aboard and hauled
my equipment up. According to my computer, I'd been
down fifty-six minutes.

I hauled the anchor aboard, coiling the line in the bow,
before starting the motor. The sea breeze had picked up

while I was under, and it blew from the east. With the motor running about three-quarters open, I pointed the bow toward the island.

The ride back took almost two hours, and during the journey, I laid out all my gear to dry in the sun. When I got back to *Carina*, I'd need to wash everything with fresh water and let it dry again.

I steered the dinghy into the channel on the western side of Isla Mujeres. The water leading up to El Milagro Marina was deep enough, but habits kept me inside the markers.

When I spotted the tall mast of *Carina*, I slowed the motor down until there was no wake coming off the outboard. I nudged up against the Tartan's hull and reached out to grab the gunwale and loop the stern line to the cleat. Once secured, I turned off the motor and raised it out of the water.

After unloading my scuba gear, I stood in the cockpit. My stomach grumbled again. It had been giving me hunger pangs since I'd gotten out of the water.

"Excuse me," a feminine voice called, pulling me from the thoughts of food and chores.

I glanced over to the dock where a woman with long brown hair stared at me. My left eyebrow lifted with curiosity at her.

"Are you Chase Gordon?"

6

The round face stared at me with amber eyes. She appeared to be in her early thirties with a dark complexion that she seemed to be born with. She didn't dress for the tropics either. Instead, she wore jeans and a baggy shirt that she likely intended to hide her curves.

Her hands rested on her hips as if she was waiting for me to answer.

"Are you Chase Gordon?" she asked again.

Nothing about her screamed CIA, and I expected that after I turned down Smith, he'd return to make another offer. The folks at Langley don't enjoy being rejected. In fact, they had the mentality that if they ask you to the dance, you'd better show up. I'd worked with several agents during my days in the Corps, and almost without exception, those agents wanted us to take all the risk while they took credit. When I was an active-duty Marine, that was acceptable. I didn't don the tan and brown fatigues for any glory. But now, I didn't have to answer some inane call to duty because some pencil-pusher told me it was my obligation.

This woman looked like a civilian. In fact, she exuded an annoyed vibe with a hint of sadness or confusion. Either of those emotions stood a better chance at stirring my sense of responsibility than some weasel like Andrew Smith.

Then again, that might be her intent.

"Who are you?" I questioned.

"My name is Danielle Traylor," she explained.

I furrowed my brow. "Ms. Traylor, do I know you?"

"Are you Chase Gordon?" she asked for the third time, and I wondered if she might be a process server attempting to get me to prove my identity before serving me with papers. Was that sort of thing even legal in Mexico?

"Yes. Now, you are..."

"I'm sorry," she blathered. "My father—uh, he and my sister were on the boat you saw."

Again, my face contorted with some confusion.

"What?"

"The *Serendipity's Odyssey*," she explained.

"Yeah, I'm sorry," I stammered. "I knew what you meant. Only, I wasn't expecting—"

The statement hung in the air. What I didn't finish saying was that I wasn't expecting any of the family to show up. It had taken me by surprise that she'd shown up. The next question hit me. Why did she come around? It put me on edge, and I backtracked in my brain. What if she were here at Smith's behest?

There was no tactful way to question the validity of her statement. At least not without coming across as a royal asshole.

"Listen, Mrs. Traylor," I replied, testing her response.

"It's Miss," she corrected me.

"Miss Traylor, I'm sorry for your loss. I just got back from a dive. Would you give me a few minutes to get cleaned up and dressed?"

"Oh, I'm sorry I interrupted you," she said. "I wasn't trying to interrupt you."

She had sad eyes. They were pretty, but sorrowful.

Always with the brown-eyed girls, Gordon.

It's not that I have a type, but one could call it a predilection. The first girl I ever fell head over heels for had brown eyes. That made me wonder though if it was because of that fifteen-year-old round-faced cutie, I was a sucker for that pigment. Or had Van Morrison brainwashed me at an early age? Or was I naturally attracted to them? It was a whole chicken or egg scenario.

"No, it's not a big deal," I assured her. "Listen, I'm starving. I planned to head into town and find some food. Have you had lunch?"

She shook her head. "No, I just got in on the morning ferry."

I nodded. "Give me ten minutes, if you don't mind."

"Okay," she responded in a demure tone. The voice seemed to match the eyes. I wasn't sure how to describe it, but there was a soft, throaty sound to it. However, Miss Traylor spoke in a hushed voice that seemed unsure of itself. I wondered if she ever sang.

While I considered that, I went into the cabin. I had stripped off my Sharkskin in the dinghy, leaving me in only my swimsuit. Once below deck, I shed the shorts and grabbed a clean pair before deciding between an old

Corps t-shirt and a casual fishing button-down. As I chose the cleaner light green fishing shirt, the actual decision I arrived at was that I needed to upgrade some of my wardrobe. The nicest clothes I had were the black shirt and pants I wore when I was working at the Manta Club back in West Palm. But those were in a box in the storage unit at the Tilly Inn and Marina, where I keep a slip.

Before climbing back on deck, I grabbed a brush and ran it through my hair, pulling free the tangles and knots acquired from the salt water and boat ride. I'd let my head get shaggy over the last year. In part, I wanted to vary my appearance. Especially after the incident in Cuba that Smith referenced. I'd pissed off some bad people, including both the Russian and Cuban governments. While I wasn't certain they knew who I was, I thought a little rougher look might disguise me.

"Are you hungry?" I asked, stepping off *Carina* and landing on the wooden pier.

"Yes," she answered before extending her hand. "Mr. Gordon, I'm so sorry to disturb you."

I took her hand. "How about you never call me Mr. Gordon? That's what people called my grandfather, and he was a giant dick."

"No one ever called you that?" she questioned.

I shook my head. "Not without being satirical. In the Marines I was a lot of things, but most people prefaced it with my rank, unless they called me by my call sign."

"What rank were you?"

"When I left the service about three years ago, I was a lieutenant."

"Anyone who would serve their country deserves to be honored," she offered.

"I could tell you it's just a job, but that would be a lie. There's nothing special about me. The only reason I joined up was to escape my life. After my first go, I liked it. So, I stayed on."

She nodded.

"I just got here yesterday, but I saw a bar next door that I'd planned on trying," I told her. "It's the Soggy Peso"

"That's cute," she commented.

I almost shrugged. She made me a little self-conscious. This woman seemed sad, but not in the way one grieves for the dead. However, if she was something more than she was pretending, it was taking her a bit to get to the hook.

Or she's damned good.

That was always the possibility. I'd wait until we got to the bar to either let her ask me what she wanted, or I'd dig a little deeper into her story.

We walked up to the street and headed north. A green sign with a hand pointing down the gravel drive read "Soggy Peso." I turned and let the limestone rock crunch under my sandals. Danielle Traylor kept up with me, not saying a word. I wondered if she was thinking the same things as me—wait until we settle at the bar. Or was she trying to build up her nerve?

Or putting you at unease.

We passed a turquoise building with a long Spanish name. I thought it said that it was a fish production site. Although, I imagine it meant something entirely different.

The next sign I understood. A hand-painted notice read in white letters, "We hope you've been overserved."

I motioned for Miss Traylor to step through the door to the patio. She chose a table with her back to the ocean. I settled opposite her in the plastic chair. Single-page menus stuck out from the napkin holder, and I smiled when I saw they were in English. My eyes landed on the Kick-Ass Shrimp Ceviche and Mexican Cheese Nachos.

A young woman in her twenties arrived, and I ordered another beer from the local brewer, a blond ale called *Claro Que Si*, and the ceviche. Danielle Traylor ordered a margarita and the bean dip.

"What can I do for you, Miss Traylor?" I asked after the waitress left the table.

"Truthfully, I don't guess I know," she replied with a shrug.

My chair tilted back as I leaned back, lifting the front legs while appraising her. In the fifteen minutes I'd known her, she traveled up and down the emotional spectrum. Although she never hit the extremes of laughing or crying, her face displayed an array of other things. At this instance, it was trepidation and doubt, as if approaching me now concerned her.

"You said it was your father's boat?" I questioned. My words were deliberate. Even though I saw little grief in her face, I didn't want to trigger her.

She nodded. "He and my sister were on board."

"I'm sorry," I told her again. There's not much one can say to a person who loses a family member. Nothing anyone says ever eases the pain. Even time can only do so much.

"Thank you," she replied in her demure tone.

I stared at her for a second. "I'm not sure what I can tell you, though."

"Do you know if they were alone?" she asked.

With a shrug, I shook my head. "I only spoke to someone on the radio. We didn't exchange names, so I'm not even sure if it was the captain or your father."

As I finished the sentence, a thought occurred to me. "You don't know if they had a crew?"

"I haven't spoken to my father in ten years," she explained.

"Oh," I remarked, understanding now her emotional reactions. I hadn't spoken to my father in longer than that. If I found out today that he'd passed away, there'd be nothing but relief.

"People always want to know why," she told me, as if confused I hadn't asked that question.

"Not my concern," I replied. "I'll assume you had justification."

She nodded. "He was not a good man."

"Neither was mine, Miss Traylor," I assured her.

"Call me Dani," she said as the waitress returned to the table with my beer and her margarita.

"My father had—let's say—boundary issues," Dani iterated. When my head cocked, she clarified, "He raped me the first time when I was fourteen."

My eyebrows raised, but I didn't reply.

Dani continued, "That continued until I was eighteen. I left home for college, planning never to come back."

"Where was your mother?" I asked.

"She killed herself when I was six. At least, that's the official story. She jumped off the back of my father's yacht."

She called it her father's yacht, not the boat or the family's yacht.

"You don't think she did it?" I wondered.

"If you knew my father, you'd wonder the same thing," she suggested. "Even if he didn't do it, he drove her to it."

"And your sister? Did you talk to her still?"

"Yes, but just recently," she answered. "We would email or message on Facebook, but we hadn't talked in over a year."

"She's younger than you?"

Dani nodded. "Three years."

I wanted to ask a question, but paused.

"By the time I left, he'd taken her to bed with him," she answered, knowing what I wondered.

"She didn't leave him then?"

The woman shook her head. Her brown eyes appeared to swell, but no tears came from them. It made me curious if she'd cried those tears long ago. Now she was in a different place. Or maybe they'd come back soon to haunt her. Regret had a way of rearing its ugly head at the least opportune times.

"Your father had money?" I asked.

She chuckled. "That's putting it mildly."

I pursed my lips.

"Have you ever heard of Traylor Technologies?"

My head shook.

"He manufactured bombs."

With that, I sat up straighter. "Bombs?"

"Yeah," she answered. "For the military."

"Excuse me," a voice interrupted us. "Ms. Traylor."

I turned my head to see two men standing about three feet from our table.

"We need you to come with us."

7

These two were what one would get if they ordered goons off the internet. Both had enough facial scars to mark them as brawlers. Those types didn't mind getting hit, and they often reveled in the injuries like they were some badges of honor. In the service, I'd seen more than a few guys like that who considered themselves tough because they didn't mind taking a punch. Their entire strategy in a fight was endurance and fear. Often their opponents tapped out simply out of caution for what they might do to them.

That didn't make them tough, though. Not really. A jackhammer can punch through concrete, but it's not about to outthink me. These two were the embodiment of a jackhammer. I guessed they were more effective together than separately.

"Do you know them?" I asked Dani.

"No," she answered.

I nodded. "Do you want to go with them?"

Dani studied them, and if she came to the same conclusion as I did, she worried that neither Jack nor Hammer had the best intent for her.

"No," she stammered, glancing back at me with worry in her eyes.

"Guys, we just ordered lunch," I explained, turning my body to face them without rising out of the white plastic chair.

"You'll have to eat it alone," Jack, the one on the left, replied.

"But she doesn't want to go with you," I explained. "And she still has her margarita."

Hammer stepped toward me. His shoulders stiffened as if he was spreading out to intimidate me.

I didn't flinch. It was bad form to do that kind of thing. People like Jack and Hammer here might not recognize me for what I am. After all, Marines don't flinch.

Of course, Hammer didn't strike me as the thinking type, so he might not take the second or two to realize they did not intimidate me. Brutes like that just assumed everyone feared them.

When I didn't react, Hammer growled and grabbed me by the front of my shirt, jerking me out of the seat. I heard the fabric rip and watched a button out of the corner of my eye as it soared off my shirt.

My left hand caught the bottle of blond ale as Hammer dragged me to my feet. With an upward jab, I drove the mouth and neck of the bottle into Hammer's throat.

He let out a guttural gasp as the blow stymied his air pipe. On instinct, the man released me as both hands flew up to his neck as if he could pull his throat open. I grabbed his shirt instead and used it to drive my knee into his groin as I jerked him down. Unable to breathe and with his nuts in his gut, the goon doubled over before collapsing to his knees. I grabbed him by the back of the head and slammed him into the table, upending it and spraying Jack with the rest of Dani's margarita.

With the blond ale bottle still in my grip, I swung it into the side of Jack's head. The first man was still stunned, both by the sudden attack on his partner and the resulting tequila shower. While the bottle didn't break on impact, it was enough to daze him.

I grabbed Dani's hand and pulled her to her feet.

"Run!" I ordered.

She didn't need to think. Dani obeyed, sprinting for the door. I stepped back a second, planting my feet before I drove my fist into Jack's nose. The resulting crunch of cartilage told me I'd just broken the man's nose.

My knuckles ached, but I ignored them as I followed Dani out the entrance. With a quick glance over my shoulder, I surveyed the mess I left with regret. If I could come back later, I'd attempt to make it up to the waitress.

Now, though, my feet were crunching against the white gravel as I ran for the street.

"Go right!" I ordered her. If we could make it back to *Carina*, I would feel better. At least there, I knew there was a hidden compartment holding my M45 and a spare magazine.

Dani sprinted ahead, but she was lagging. I stole a look back, relieved that no one followed us out of the bar. I didn't think Hammer would be running anywhere too soon, but Jack would recover soon. He might reconsider confronting me right away, though.

"I can't," Dani gasped. Her chest heaved as she took in deep breaths.

"It's okay," I told her. "Walk."

"Sorry, I'm not in great shape."

"You did great."

"What did those guys want?" she asked me.

"Dani, I just met you," I pointed out. "I don't have a clue, but I know people. Those two were knee-breakers."

"Knee-breakers?" she repeated.

"They work for someone else, and their job is likely enforcement."

"Who?" she demanded.

"Someone wanted something from you," I suggested as we turned into the lot at El Milagro.

"How did they find me?" she asked. "And why?"

"Where are you staying?"

"I'm staying on the mainland. I planned on catching the ferry back this afternoon."

That didn't strike me as the best idea. If I were Jack and Hammer, I'd expect her to take the ferry. Especially if they knew she was on the ferry. That seemed logical, unless they knew she was coming to talk with me.

For a second, I wondered if Jack and Hammer worked for Smith. He sent them along to stir the pot. But those two weren't government. Hell, they weren't even independent contractors. Those two worked for someone because they were too dumb to do it themselves.

"Chase!" Dani exclaimed, pointing behind me.

I spun around as Jack lumbered up the drive toward us. The black metal of a Beretta handgun appeared. As he raised it up, I recognized the 92XI model.

"I'm not fucking around," he grunted.

My hands raised in surrender. There's a stark difference between getting the drop on a guy in a fist fight and trying to punch out a nine-millimeter pistol. It's not that I couldn't disarm someone, but Jack was over ten feet away from me. Unless he closed that gap, I didn't stand a chance.

As I looked into the goon's eyes, I knew he'd shoot me, too. There was no doubt about that. Perhaps if I hadn't broken his nose. My gaze shifted to the bloody, crooked thing. It would never be straight, and while I might take some comfort in that, it wouldn't make me less dead if he pulled the trigger.

"What do you want?" I demanded, implying I still had control here.

"She's coming with me."

My head shook, and I stepped in front of her. Jack's eyes narrowed.

"Do you think I can't shoot you and take her?" he snarled.

"No, I think you'd have no problem with it," I replied. "Now, those guys over there will be nice eyewitnesses."

His eyes followed my gesture to three guys standing under the entrance to a portico with the name "El Milagro" painted above them.

"This is a small island too," I pointed out.

"So?" he barked.

"How fast can you get off the island with a girl who knows you'll probably kill her? Do you think she's just going to follow along blindly?"

"She'll do what I say," he snapped.

I made a move like I was talking over my shoulder. "Will you, Dani?" I asked. "Or will you scream and fight to stay safe?"

"I'm going to fucking bite the asshole," she stated in the boldest voice I'd heard come from her lips.

"Good girl," I replied, before turning my attention back to Jack. "She will not be so easy to get out of here, and I figure by now the cops have been called. Don't forget what I said, 'This is a small island.'"

He stared down the barrel of the 92XI, and I thought he might just shoot me. Somehow, he seemed to consider it. He glanced back at the street—looking for Hammer. That would solve his problems. Two of them could control Dani.

"Even with your buddy, how do you plan to get her off the island?" I asked.

"Shut up, I'm done talking to you," he stated.

He blinked, and I knew he was pulling the trigger. The flash of pink startled him, and he jerked the barrel down as he fired. The bullet slapped into the asphalt in front of me, spewing bits of tar and rock up.

Jack jerked around as the pink golf cart careened through the driveway. An old man spun the wheel away from the man with the gun, but he'd been running the cart fast. The sudden turn brought the vehicle's forward momentum to a stop as it slid sideways. Inertia pushed the top-heavy cart on, and the left wheels lifted off the pavement.

The next two seconds ticked by in slow motion as the cart rolled sideways with a crash. Jack flew back as the roof slammed into him. In the driver's seat of the cart, the old man, having had the good sense to fasten the seat belt, hung in the seat sideways. As everything came to a stop, I saw the man's face. A toothless grin beamed off him.

"Go!" I shouted, urging Dani to run.

Adrenaline drove her forward, and she raced through the portico toward the marina. Behind her, I peered back to see Jack picking himself up. The three men who'd been watching the scene charged forward, and I realized the gunman had dropped his Beretta.

Dani's feet clomped along the wooden pier, and I hurried around her. It wouldn't take long for Jack to get past those men, and I hoped none of them got injured.

As I passed the bowline attaching *Carina* to the dock, I uncoiled it from the cleat and tossed it onto the deck. Dani grabbed my hand and climbed aboard.

"Get below deck!" I ordered, as I uncoiled the stern line.

When I stepped aboard, I pushed the boat away from the dock. I'd tied *Carina* alongside the long pier, and now I only needed to get the engine started and pull away. *Carina* fired up with the twist of the key, and I was shifting her into gear as I spun the wheel.

The diesel engine didn't push her fast, but it did chug us away from the dock fast enough. I let out a sigh as I saw Jack barrel down the pier toward us. We were already twenty feet off the dock, and I aimed the bow away from shore before scrambling through the cockpit to jump down the companionway.

I heard the gunshots as Jack fired at our retreating stern. Dani curled up in a ball on the floor as I jumped over her and reached under the port settee. Behind my black water tank was a small compartment that looked like it was part of the poop tank. I retrieved my forty-five-caliber pistol and went back on deck.

We were now almost three hundred feet from the dock, but I kept my head down. Unless Jack was a crack shot, it was unlikely he'd hit me. Still, no point in making it easy for him.

He stood on the dock, shouting at us. I glanced behind to see my inflatable dinghy dragging along at an awkward angle. Then I realized it was because one tube sported a gash, leaving it deflated.

The fucker shot my dinghy!

8

Dani hadn't come back out of the cabin. When I stepped below, I found her curled on the cushions, asleep. The adrenaline crash and shock from the attack knocked her out. I left her to sleep it off. There wasn't much she could do now, and it was getting late in the afternoon.

In the cockpit, I motored south along the coastline, staying about a mile offshore. There were only a few marinas on this little island, and I didn't think any of those would harbor us for long. The two thugs would be searching for us to make land somewhere.

The southern tip of Isla Mujeres was a national park with no easy access to the shore. Certainly not for guys like Jack and Hammer, whose idea of roughing it was driving down gravel roads. *Carina* slipped into a cove surrounded by jungle. I lowered the forty-five-pound Rocna anchor until the hook settled in the sand. I reversed the motor just enough to pull against the taut rode and dig the ground tackle into the ocean floor. Once I felt it was secure, I let out about fifty feet of chain, allowing *Carina* to swing in the inlet.

My stomach still grumbled, having missed out on the ceviche and nachos I'd promised it at Soggy Peso. I hadn't restocked the galley since my plan was to spend two days at El Milagro. There was no bread and no lunchmeat left, and only a six-pack of warm beer in the cabinet. Luckily, I found a can of fruit cocktail and some ravioli. The pasta heated up in its original container on my grill while I devoured the syrupy fruit. Once the ravioli was hot, I leaned back in the cockpit and spooned the soft noodles into my mouth. Not exactly gourmet, but it did the trick.

My M45 sat in the compartment beside the helm. I didn't expect the two goons to find a boat and come looking for us, but I didn't want to rule it out. It didn't seem like either of them would grasp what to do on a boat, but it would be a mistake to take that for granted.

It left me wondering what they wanted with Dani. I assumed that what she told me was the truth. It was possible the entire thing was a scheme to trap me, but my gut told me she was honest with me. It's hard to fake fear, and I'd seen her face. Those two goons scared her.

The sun went down, and I sipped on the last beer from my fridge. A fishing boat zoomed nearby, and I perked up, watching it until it sped past. Just another fisherman heading back from a late afternoon trip. After some time, I counted stars in the dark purple sky. I had brought a blanket into the cockpit, not because the air chilled me. It would provide me a shield from the mosquitoes thriving in the jungle wrapping around this cove.

RED LIGHT AT NIGHT

"Chase?" Dani's voice pulled me from my slumber. I straightened up, reaching over on instinct to touch the grip of the M45.

"Yeah, I'm up here," I called down to her.

The companionway doors swung open, and she stepped out. "I'm sorry I passed out."

I offered her a smile, telling her, "It's all right. That was quite an afternoon."

"Where are we?" she asked, surveying the dark.

"I dropped anchor on the southwest side of the island. No one should be able to find us here. Not without approaching by boat."

"Thank you," she muttered. "You've done too much."

I smiled back. Now she was more relaxed, and her already soft features almost glowed in the night air.

"Do you need something to eat?" I asked.

She shook her head. "No, I'm fine. But I don't have any clothes."

There were some shirts and a bikini that Missy left on board, but none of them would fit Dani. "There should be a t-shirt and some shorts of mine down below."

"You think I can squeeze into them?" she remarked. "I've got a lot of boobs."

My eyebrow raised, and I held my tongue. I stood up and climbed below, pulling the Marine Corps shirt I'd considered wearing earlier and a pair of running shorts from the drawer in the v-berth.

"I'll give you a minute," I promised her as I headed for the steps to the cockpit. When I passed the galley, I paused and removed a bottle of rum and two glasses before heading on deck.

After settling back into the cockpit, I poured three ounces of the dark-brown Jamaican rum into the glasses. My internal clock told me it was after midnight.

The doors opened, and she stepped into the night air. The glow from my solar lanterns cast shadows around the cockpit. I tried not to glance at her but failed as my eyes swept as discreetly as possible over her. Dani held her arms over her midriff, crossing them.

"Here, I hope you like rum," I said, offering her the glass of aged brown rum.

She took the proffered drink and smiled. "How did you know I needed one?"

"It's been a bit of a day," I suggested. "I'm assuming you aren't in the habit of being accosted and chased across foreign countries?"

"I've never escaped in a boat before. Unless you count Spring Break in my sophomore year."

"Not sure that I'd count that, although I didn't experience the dangers of college."

She sipped the glass. "You didn't go to college?" she asked.

"Not traditionally. I joined the Marines when I was eighteen—technically seventeen. I went back to school but while I was on active duty. Never got the degree, though."

"How long were you in the Corps?"

"Long enough, and nowhere near long enough."

She nodded as if she understood me. "What did you do?"

"I worked my way in to Recon, and most of those missions are classified."

"Like the Rangers?" she questioned.

"Like the Rangers, if they were meaner, tougher, and more reliant."

She laughed half-heartedly at that.

I took a sip and realized her glass was empty. As I raised the bottle in my hand, I offered her another. She extended her glass and left it until I'd filled it over halfway.

"What made you come looking for me?" I asked her as she gulped the rum. "You might want to slow down."

"Why? Are you going to take advantage of me?" she asked. Her eyes glittered in the starlight and soft glow of the solar lanterns.

"Dani, I never take advantage of women," I promised her in what I hoped was an equally flirtatious tone. "It's usually the other way around."

As if to confuse me more, she shifted the tone back to answer my question. "My sister, Carlee, messaged me three days ago." I nodded, taking a drink of the rum to avoid asking questions. I wanted to hear her story from her perspective and without any interference from me.

"She and my father," she used the term with the same emotion one might offer to their lawyer, "have been together now for ten years. Carlee didn't go into a lot of details about their life—thank goodness. But she said some things about the business. He'd been running something secretive, even from Carlee."

"Was that unusual?" I questioned now.

"It seemed so," Dani answered. "Carlee was the Chairwoman of the Board, so she should have been privy to even the top-secret work. But she said Dad was working some deal behind her back."

"Did she say what it might have been?" I asked, wondering what it was and how the CIA was involved. If Traylor built weapons, the reason for the CIA's interest made sense.

It piqued more questions. If Traylor Technologies built weapons for the government, the company's leaders would have undergone some serious vetting. How would they miss an incestuous relationship between the father and daughter, both officers of the company?

"She didn't know," Dani answered. "It's what worried her. She thought he might be doing something illegal."

"What did she expect you to do?" I wondered. "You haven't talked to her in years."

"I thought that maybe she wanted me to report him. She didn't say that, but she made a few comments like, 'What can I do?'"

"If you reported him, then you'd be reporting her," I pointed out. "Even if she wasn't aware of what he was doing, guilt by association would drag her down, too."

"That might have been better than turning on my father," she suggested.

"Oh," I said with understanding. "I get that."

She stared at me with some contemplation.

"My father was abusive," I explained. "Mine never sexually abused me, but he beat me and my siblings relentlessly."

"What happened to him?" she asked. Anticipation filled her eyes.

"He's not dead," I remarked. "He's serving thirty years in a prison in Arkansas for murdering my brother."

"Oh," she whispered. Her hand reached over to touch my arm. I didn't need the comfort, but the soft touch of her fingers felt electric on my skin. I reached over and put my hand on top of hers with a gentle squeeze.

"Did you report him?" I asked, trying to focus on what we'd already talked about. It was difficult to concentrate with my hand and hers still touching.

She shook her head in a slow motion. Her eyes remained locked on mine. Dani leaned forward, sliding to the edge of the bench. The night breeze came off the shore carrying a hint of sea grapes along with it. Waves lapped against the hull with no pattern. All of that seemed to meld into a microcosm.

"I couldn't," she responded. "Does that make sense? Like as much as I hated him for everything he did to me, I didn't have the courage to stand up to him. It was easier to run away."

With a nod, I replied, "I understand that."

"Your father?" she asked.

I nodded. There's more to the story, but I'd learned to deal with it. As long as Gerald Gordon was in prison, my coping mechanisms worked. If one day, the State of Arkansas deemed he'd served his time, then that method might need to be reworked.

"You got away, though," I pointed out, guiding us back onto the subject of her family.

"As soon as I could. He cut me off once he realized I would not come back."

"What did you do?" I asked her, leaning closer.

"While my dad cut me off, that didn't leave me without money. I had a trust from my mother that I used to move to London, where I worked with Care for Peace."

My eyebrows furrowed, and she added, "It's a non-profit."

"I've heard of them," I replied. What I didn't add was that the organization didn't have the best standing among the military and government leaders. Of course, any group whose primary goal was the complete disarming of the world might not be held in high regards among the ones making all the money off war. Personally, I have mixed feelings. In a perfect world, war wouldn't be necessary; and the US government spends far too much on armaments when it could use some of that money elsewhere. At the same time, it's not a perfect world. I'd like to think that violence wasn't inherent in me, but that was not the case. It might not be the first thing I use, but it remained in my arsenal.

Dani must have read my mind. She commented, "I'm not against the military."

I didn't respond.

She continued, "I was specifically against him, and no one would go up against my father. After all, he had the last three presidents on speed dial. And they didn't put him on hold, if you know what I mean."

I nodded. If that were true, then Dani's father had a great deal of sway.

"CFP didn't mind going up against him. It was a losing battle, but for CFP it was publicity. That garnered donations."

"It would still cost them to go to court, wouldn't it?"

She shook her head but replied, "Yes, but enough cases settle out of court that CFP can fund their legal battles off those small winnings. I think they sue for things they know will draw the publicity to get companies to settle quickly."

"It seems like a scam," I commented.

She pulled her hand away and finished her glass. "Isn't everything?" she asked.

I shrugged. "Sitting here isn't."

She extended the glass for me to fill up. After it was full, she clinked her glass against mine. "Isn't it?" she asked.

Confused, I replied, "What?"

"Isn't it a scam?" she asked, moving across the cockpit to sit next to me on the port bench.

"It doesn't feel like it," I stammered. Or at least I began to say it. However, she leaned in toward me, and I closed the distance. When we kissed, I inhaled the taste of dark rum on her breath. Her full lips caressed mine, and, like an addict, I wanted more. As I leaned forward, she pushed away gently, keeping her lips just out of reach of mine until my brain caught up to the rest of my body.

I didn't pull away, but I relaxed back. She followed my body and still seemed to lead me back until she pressed me against the hull. Dani took my glass in my hand and put it to my lips, pouring the rest of the rum in my mouth. When a drop ran off my lip, she swept in and kissed it off me.

Dani leaned back and drank her glass of rum before setting both empty tumblers on the helm. She straddled my lap, and I stared up at the green shirt I'd worn around the boat a hundred times. I only had a split second to admire her in my shirt before she leaned over and kissed me again. Without the glass of rum in my hand, I slid all ten fingers along her hips and across her back.

She straightened up and stared at me with those dark amber eyes that seemed to widen. Dani's mouth turned up into a soft smile.

"I've been wanting to do that since I saw you," she moaned.

"Me too," I admitted.

The half smile on her face brightened into a gleam, and she took her hands and pulled the bottom of the Marine Corps shirt over her head, exposing her bare breasts.

I felt the smile spread across my face, and she bent over to kiss me again.

9

The boat creaked as she rocked in the waves. I lifted my head slowly to find Dani nestled against my bare chest. Sunlight filtered through the shaded portholes, and the internal clock in my head told me it was a few minutes past seven.

Dani squirmed, and her naked breast rubbed against me. Her left leg draped over me. She lay comfortably snuggled against me. I inhaled to breathe in the smell of citrus that came from her skin. We had slept little, having moved from the cockpit, where I hoped I'd find a wad of our clothes on the deck, to the salon. Sometime around five, we ended up in the forward berth where we fell asleep.

The anchor chain groaned as *Carina* pulled against the hook. While I thought I should get up and make sure that the increasing wind wasn't dragging us across the ocean floor, I didn't want to. Besides, I knew I had a solid tackle. Since I'd upgraded to the heavier Rocna, *Carina* hadn't dragged an inch. No point in assuming she would now.

Instead, I wrapped my arm around Dani, relishing the sensation of heat from her supple skin. Her bare shoulders hadn't seen a lot of sunlight. Not surprising if she'd been living in London. I'd need to make sure she protected herself if she was going to be in the Mexican sun. It's a different world from England.

"Are you awake?" she murmured.

"Yeah," I replied.

She craned her neck to look up at me. Her round lips curled into a smile, and she pushed up to kiss me.

"What time is it?" she asked when she pulled her face away from mine.

"About twenty past seven."

"What time did we get to bed?" she wondered aloud.

"To bed?" I asked. "Or to sleep?"

Dani giggled. "To sleep."

"A little past five."

"You only got a couple of hours of sleep," she pointed out. "I'm sorry I kept you up."

With a laugh, I assured her, "That is nothing to be sorry about."

Her grin remained. "Good. I liked it."

"Me too," I admitted.

"Chase," she said my name with a cautious tone. "There's something I should have told you before we—uh—before last night."

"Are you married?" I joked.

"Not yet," she answered. Her response was flat, and I tilted my chin to study her.

Her wide, round eyes stared at me.

"Not yet?" I questioned.

"I'm engaged."

"Ah," I muttered.

"It wasn't fair of me not to tell you," she remarked. "But I think it was the rush of emotions."

Pushing back, I slid out from under her and sat up. "Look, Dani, I didn't ask either."

"It's just that—"

"Oh, I get it, Dani. It's not like my life is set up for entanglements," I stated, regretting it as soon as the words left my lips.

"What does that mean?" she snapped.

"Whoa, I didn't mean it badly," I attempted to explain, realizing as I spoke I was making things worse. "I don't have anyone in my life. Not because I don't want it. For most of my life, I did what someone told me to do. Now, I do what I want. Most people aren't up for that spur-of-the-moment lifestyle."

"I wasn't asking to join your pirate crew," Dani retorted. "It was only sex. But I should have told you beforehand. It happened quicker than I expected."

My head cocked a bit. "You started it," I pointed out.

"Yeah," she admitted. "I didn't think you'd respond." She let out a heavy sigh.

"What did you expect me to do?" I asked. "I'm not a monk, and if someone I find attractive and I like kisses me, I kiss back. That seems like an appropriate response."

"I like you too," she replied.

"Why?" I questioned.

"Why do I like you?"

"No, why did you make the move?" I clarified.

"Uh, I don't know. After yesterday, I realized that if I'd been in the same situation with Clayton, he'd never react the same way as you."

"That's a spotty reason, at best," I pointed out.

"No, it's shitty of me," she said. "It's unfair to you and him."

I sat on the bunk, staring at her. She straightened up, and I strained not to stare at her naked form. Not that looking her in the face was better. Her amber eyes drilled into me.

"Okay," I finally said. "I'm a big boy."

"Chase," she pleaded.

"Dani, it's fine. I don't expect anything," I assured her, aware that my words came out hollow, at least to me. Still, I continued, "The longest relationship I've had is with a married woman. Might be my fault. A psychologist would say I sought unavailable women."

She stared at me for a few seconds. "I'm not unavailable," she explained, breaking the silence.

"Engaged is pretty close," I suggested. For the first time, I glanced at her hand that moved to cover her breasts without any thought. There was no ring. Not even the indention of where one had been.

"Except for telling him, it's over."

I shook my head. "Dani, I like you, but so far, we've known each other for less than twenty-four hours. I've got a piece of fish in the fridge I've had longer than that."

Dani rolled her eyes. "What did I say? There's no way I'm joining your crew."

We locked eyes for a split second before she cracked a smile. I couldn't help but smile back.

"Clayton and I should have ended it already," she told me. "After yesterday—and last night—I did what I needed for me."

I nodded. "What is that?"

"In case you hadn't noticed yet, I'm a fucking mess. Hell, I'm probably the poster child for Daddy Issues." She stiffened her back, pulling her hands away from her chest as if she was taunting me. "I think I need to just be."

I nodded again.

She added, "Assuming I can survive the next day or so."

The comment reminded me of the immediate problem. I couldn't drop her off on the dock. Someone was after her. Two someones, at the least.

Way to complicate shit.

"We need to figure that out," I said.

"How?"

I considered Andrew Smith. Would he have a vested interest in protecting Dani?

Not likely. The CIA only had a vested interest in helping itself.

"Why did you come to Isla Mujeres?" I asked.

"When I got the call the other day that my father's boat went down, I knew something was off. Carlee had just sent me a message and then she's dead. That made little sense to me. We hadn't spoken more than a few emails in a decade and now—this. How does that make sense?"

"Coincidences happen," I advised her.

"Do they?" she wondered aloud.

"I suppose," I countered with little conviction. "The problem with them is they are unpredictable, and generally, they are a statistical improbability. So, I don't buy them."

"Exactly," she declared.

"Your sister messages you that your father is up to something, and you think she might have wanted you to report it. Then, a day or so later, they are both dead."

"It doesn't sit well with me."

I nodded. "You want to know what doesn't sit well with me?"

She stared at me with rapt attention.

"In thousands of square miles of open water, I come across a single vessel, and it blows up while I'm watching it."

"You think they wanted to drag you into it?"

"At the least, they wanted a witness," I suggested. "Boats go missing every year. I think I read that last year it was in the upper forties. Most of the time, no one knows what happened to them. It might take time to determine that the boat has sunk and not just incommunicado. Even after that, it takes time to declare the crew missing and then dead. We're talking years."

Dani leaned forward, intent on my words.

I continued, "Unless they have a witness."

"Oh shit," she muttered. "They wanted someone to see the yacht going down."

"Not just that," I added. "They wanted me to identify it."

"Why?" she questioned.

"By the time I finished with the Coast Guard, they probably had a preliminary report typed and transmitted to their command, setting in motion the events happening after any death. Such as notifying the next of kin and sometimes associates."

Dani considered this for a minute.

"Who has control of Traylor Technologies now?"

"I don't know," she confessed.

"Okay, you came looking for answers, but why here?" I asked. "Your father's yacht was never here. He sailed out of Cozumel."

"The man with the Coast Guard told me you were coming here."

My eyes narrowed. That was possible. After all, I'd told the ensign who took my statement what my itinerary was, in case he needed anything. However, it seemed highly unusual to me.

"Was this the same person who reported the explosion to you?"

She nodded.

"When did this happen?" I asked.

"Tuesday morning."

"You were in London?"

Again, she nodded.

"What time?"

Dani thought about it and answered, "About six. The call woke me up."

"That's too fast."

"What do you mean?" she asked.

"If they called you at six, that was about midnight for me. The Coasties had only just shown up. There's no way they could identify you that soon."

"So, it wasn't the Coast Guard?"

I shook my head. "No, it wasn't. Whoever you talked to was involved in killing your father and sister."

"Why?" she demanded.

That wasn't the question I had. Had whoever killed Dani's family targeted me before I met *Serendipity's Odyssey* at sea, or was I just a convenience?

In my head, I did the calculations. There would be almost no way of predicting exactly what heading I was taking, and if I'd changed my course by even a degree from the onset, it could put me miles away from the path of *Serendipity's Odyssey*. Add in any alteration in course by Dani's father, and the odds skyrocketed.

Unless someone on *Serendipity's Odyssey* steered the yacht toward me. It wouldn't be difficult to find me on the open water. I was running my AIS, and anyone can track, at least, a yacht's general vicinity from multiple vessel-tracking websites. But it would require the captain to arrange the rendezvous—which would be suicide.

Or it could be they opted for the first ship to pass in the night.

"We need to get ahead of this," I commented.

"How?" she asked.

"Your father and sister must have been into something," I explained. "The CIA visited me the day before you arrived."

"CIA?"

I nodded.

"What did they want?" she inquired.

"I'm not exactly sure. He asked me to look into what happened to your father's yacht."

"Did he say why?"

"No, but then I didn't give him much chance before I said no."

"But now you will?" Dani asked.

"I have some questions now that need answers," I explained.

"What do we do?"

"Your father and sister left Cozumel Tuesday morning. If someone planted an explosive on the yacht, that would be the most likely place it happened. We start there and find out what we can."

"Cozumel? Do we just sail there?"

"It will take us a day or so."

She blinked her eyes at me. "Do we have to leave right now?" Her fingers extended out to stroke down my chest.

"I'm in no rush," I assured her.

"Good," she replied, pushing up on her arms to bring her face toward mine.

Our lips touched, and she pressed me back into the mattress with her naked form.

10

By the time I saw the lights of Cozumel, it was after nine in the evening. The stars spread across the sky, and despite the moon's absence, the visibility at night offered us about a mile. With a steady breeze off the beam, we made decent time. Although, I would have preferred to come into a new marina in the daylight.

This wasn't Dani's first time on the sea. She told stories about going out on her father's boat when she was a girl. She stretched out on the starboard side of the cockpit. While the sun was up, she remained under the dodger, saying her pale skin wouldn't fare well in the bright sun. I offered her ample supplies of high SPF sunscreen. In turn, I got to watch her apply it.

Despite having lost her immediate family, Dani didn't appear to be grieving. From what she'd said, those feelings happened long ago, and their deaths just punctuated the loss. I doubted I'd have a different reaction if I found out my father had died. Since I'd vowed to kill the man myself if I ever saw him again, it seemed unlikely I'd feel anything for him. The sooner he was off the face of the earth, the better the world would be.

Now, the chartplotter mapped me through the dark harbor to the lights of Marina Puerto de Abrigo. Red and green lights littered the black water ahead. A few bright white lights indicated boats floating at anchor. I guided *Carina* through the dark. The danger out here was a boat running without lights. It was illegal, but some of the local fishermen worked little pangas that zipped around with low profiles and small outboards. Hopefully, I'd hear one buzzing across the surface, but if it were just drift fishing, I might plow right over them.

As we sailed closer to shore, I started the diesel engine, leaving the throttle in neutral. If I needed to react, I could shift the transmission into gear and the motor would take over control of the Tartan's forward momentum.

The lights of the port grew closer. Whenever I headed into a new port, especially at night, it felt like a long time from when I first spotted the lights until I could make out the details.

"What are we going to do?" Dani asked.

"We need to trace back your family's movements."

"How do we do that?" she questioned. "It's a big city, isn't it?"

"Not that big, I promise you," I assured her. "Your father had an eighty-eight-foot yacht. Those draw attention. In the boating community, people will take notice. Hell, if you get on Facebook, you can find three or four pictures in the local groups where people ask whose boat it is."

"Really? They do that?"

"We as a species are incurably curious—to the point of intrusive. Add a little envy on top of that, and there will be inquiries." I gave her a little smile, adding, "Those questions cue up the ones who want to be perceived as in the know—the gossipmongers who know everything."

Dani fished her phone out of her pocket. The screen lighted up, illuminating her cheeks.

"Oh, I got a bar," she declared like an ancient sailor crying, "Land ho!"

It wasn't an addiction that enslaved me. I never carried a personal phone. When I joined the Corps, I let my cell phone plan go. After all, I wasn't carrying it on duty back then, and I was always on duty. Besides, I'd joined up to get away from everyone, so there seemed no point in providing any type of tether to let them pull me back. After the Corps shipped me off on my first tour, the most I'd do was call my sister once every couple of months. During that time, I never developed the habit of checking my phone. The people I went to high school with were doing exactly what they were doing when I left north Arkansas. I didn't care enough to check. After I got out, I found it was a lot nicer to find the out of the way places with no cell coverage. Beautiful anchorages with pristine coral reefs never have good Wi-Fi, and I remain content with that.

Back in Florida, most of my phone calls came to the Manta Club, where I bartended to fill up the cruising kitty. I expected when I got back next month, I would find a stack of messages—most from my sister.

"I'll be damned," Dani whispered.

"What?"

"I found this 'What's Happening in Cozumel' group on Facebook. There are two pictures of my father's boat on here."

"Told you," I quipped with smugness.

"Someone asks who owned the boat anchored out front of El Presidente. Then someone says it belongs to Vincent Traylor."

"Vincent?" She hadn't told me her father's name. In fact, she'd almost avoided using his name at all.

"Yeah, it even sounds evil," she remarked.

I only nodded as I moved to starboard and released the halyard, controlling the jib sail. As soon as the line came off the winch, I grabbed the drum line and reeled the sail hand over hand. The squeak of the drum turning was barely audible over the din of the sea, but the flapping sail retreated as it coiled around the sail feeder.

Carina slowed as the foresail released its wind. As soon as the clew of the jib wrapped around the rest of the sail, I released the main halyard, gripped in the cam cleat. As the mainsail dropped, any forward momentum we experienced was only because of inertia. While the sail folded into the lazy jack system, I grabbed the helm, pushing the throttle forward. The diesel engine kicked into gear with a groan as *Carina* surged forward.

It took another hour to get into the marina, and once we tied up, the overnight security guard wandered out onto the dock finger to check on us. Once assured we were supposed to be there, he left us alone for the night.

I ducked below deck and dropped onto the settee. Dani stopped in the galley, retrieving two beers. She popped the top off one and handed it to me. "I assume you can have one now," she remarked.

Taking the bottle, I nodded before putting it to my lips.

"After you finish that one, I thought we'd head back to bed," Dani suggested.

I smiled wide before turning the beer up and sucking the contents out in four large gulps. Dani stared wide-eyed at me before breaking into laughter. My hand extended, holding out the empty bottle for her. She reached over and took it from me. After setting it down, she slid over onto my lap and put her arms around me. Our lips touched, and I didn't know if it was the alcohol on my breath or hers that I tasted.

It didn't matter to me though, and as Dani arched her back, she pulled the t-shirt over her head before leaning back down to kiss me again.

11

"*Serendipity's Odyssey?*" the scruffy harbormaster repeated when I inquired about Traylor's yacht. "What was she?" He was in his forties, and while gray flecked his shaggy beard, the hair on his head was onyx. So black that I wondered if he'd colored it. That made little sense, considering he'd not done the same for his facial hair.

"A Sunseeker 88," I detailed. "She left Cozumel on Monday."

"*Era uno grande,*" he remarked. Even my pitiful Spanish understood he thought the yacht was a large one. Eighty-eight feet would take up most of the dock space in a marina like El Presidente's. As I explained to Dani, a boat that size always drew attention.

"*Lo recuerdo,*" a young male dockworker in his teens remarked. He glanced at me, noting the lack of understanding, and repeated in English, "I remember it."

The harbormaster appeared confused or, perhaps, just uninterested in volunteering any information. I guessed he expected a bribe for any tidbit, and his junior employee now derailed that train. Annoyed, he barked something at the boy, who scurried back out of the office.

"Wait," I demanded, locking eyes with the man in charge. "Let him talk," I insisted.

The dockhand grew nervous. "They anchored out," he responded.

I cut my gaze to the harbormaster, who nodded. "Yes, I remember that now," he lied. There was no chance he'd forgotten about the biggest boat in the marina.

"How long were they here?" I asked.

The older man jutted his bottom lip out and shook his head. My head turned to the young dockhand, who now realized it was in his best interest with the boss to keep his mouth shut.

"Why do you want to know?" the bearded boss asked.

"Someone blew the boat up Tuesday night," I stated in a flat voice.

"Blew it up?" the boy exclaimed.

"*¡Vuelva al trabajo!*"

The boy turned and vanished out the office door.

"What do you mean 'blew it up?'" the man asked.

I slipped a twenty-dollar bill from my pocket. While I had plenty of pesos, the locals weren't shy of the US dollar, and it always grabbed their attention. My right hand extended in a handshake.

"The name's Chase," I introduced myself as I passed him the bill.

His mouth widened, revealing yellow, chipped teeth. "Manuel," he replied.

"Someone put a bomb on *Serendipity's Odyssey*," I explained. "Since this was the last place she berthed, it's probable that someone accessed the boat here."

RED LIGHT AT NIGHT

"It wasn't us," he spouted in defense.

"Of course not," I assured him. There was little about the man or the boy I'd just met that indicated to me they could install an explosive device. Not that looks couldn't be deceiving, but my instincts suggested it was someone else.

"We do not let people on the vessels without the owners' permission," he stated, as he realized there might be some liability that fell on the marina.

"No, I know that," I replied, attempting to soothe his anxiety. "However, I don't think the culprit did so with anyone's consent."

Manuel stared at me. "What do you want from us?" He used the pronoun, "us," in order to spread out any guilt that might befall him. The marina was a corporate-owned entity, and Manuel might be worried that any blowback would cause him to become classified as the scapegoat.

"I'd like to see any video surveillance you have," I explained.

His eyebrows furrowed. "I don't think I can allow that."

That wasn't a surprise. Even in the States, I'd find it difficult to get that kind of cooperation from a business with no legal backing. Which, of course, I didn't have.

Dani, who'd been standing behind me, stepped forward, speaking for the first time since we entered the office. "Manuel, we understand that might be a problem. All we want is to sort this out as soon as possible."

"I would have to ask the manager for permission."

Dani pressed past me. Her head bobbed in a slow, rhythmic motion. "That might be good," she suggested.

"Of course, the person who did this killed at least two people. I'm sure that the management would want to know that they are doing whatever is needed to help. Our goal is just to find anything that will help lead us to the murderers."

"Murderers?" the man repeated. Manuel seemed to taste the word in his mouth.

Dani offered, "The sooner we can get a look, though, the better chance we have of preventing it from happening again."

Manuel considered this. After several seconds, he caressed the twenty-dollar bill in his hand. He toyed with the idea of requesting more, but something held him back. He might worry that if we talked to the manager, his boss would cut him out of any money.

"I can speak with my boss," he informed us. "But it might take some time." There was the squeaky wheel that needed grease.

"How soon can you get the footage?" I asked him. "We would be very grateful for any help."

His eyes lighted up as he picked up on the cue that our satisfaction might mean more money in his pocket. He evaluated us, trying to decide if he should hit us up now or wait until he had something to show us.

"How far back do you want to see?" he asked.

"At least as far back as *Serendipity's Odyssey* was in the harbor," I replied. "But the last couple of days, for sure."

"Can I have it to you by tomorrow?"

I glanced at Dani before responding with a nod. "Yes, that would be fine. Do I need to reach out to your boss?"

He shook his head. "No, *señor*, I will speak with him."

I gave him a curt nod, resisting the urge to smile at human nature. Greed worked wonders, and Manuel knew if he brought in his boss, then he might have to share any tip we gave him—if he could keep any of it at all.

"We'll be back tomorrow," I assured him.

Manuel's eyes shifted to my hands, but all I offered him was an empty handshake. No point in over-greasing a wheel. It just became excessive and messy.

Dani and I exited the marina office and strolled back across a lot.

"Want some lunch?" I asked her.

"Fat girls like to eat," she advised.

My eyes narrowed at her. I started to argue with her assessment, but prudence suggested it was a futile effort. Instead, I pointed across a well-manicured yard toward the Intercontinental Hotel. She started trotting across the grass, and I followed along.

Inside the hotel, we followed the signs toward El Caribeño. The Caribbean-style restaurant overlooked the sea. A young hostess motioned for us to follow her through a patio area that looked like a giant tiki hut. The open-air dining area peered out from under the thatched roof at clear blue waters. The melodic drone of outboard motors flowed in the air.

It was well after lunch, and most of the clientele were hotel guests living on vacation time. She seated us at a small round table near the edge of the patio. A couple sat around an unlit pyre. The melting, frozen concoctions in hurricane glasses didn't appear to be their first drink of the afternoon. The woman let out a cackle as if to signal it wasn't even her second cocktail. After all, it's always five o'clock somewhere.

The afternoon sun radiated down, reflecting off the rippled surface of the Caribbean waters. A pair of polarized sunglasses hung around my neck, and I lifted them up to rest on my nose.

"I could stay here," Dani remarked as she stared off across the blue waves.

"It's hard to hate it," I agreed as I focused on her face. "It might not be as debonair as London, but you can't knock the weather."

She smiled. "No, it's got London beat."

"Why England?" I asked. "It seems like you could work for Care for Peace from anywhere."

"Come on, there's something magical about London," she explained. "It's like an unpolished gemstone. There are glints of possibilities throughout it, but this dull sheen hides it. There's the bustle of a metropolis combined with this odd quaintness. Or maybe I'm still enthralled like a dumb American."

I grinned as a dark-skinned girl approached the table. Dani ordered a frozen daiquiri, and I opted for a Tecate in a bottle.

"Do you think we'll see anything in the video?" she asked.

I almost shook my head. It was a wild grasp at straws. If *Serendipity's Odyssey* had tied up to the pier, the chances were better. Even then, I could have snuck aboard with little fear of being spotted. But since they anchored the yacht a hundred feet from the docks, gaining access without crossing paths with a camera angle would be easy. I could make my way underwater, slipping onto the boat in the dead of night. If it was just Dani's father and sister, then avoiding contact was a cinch. Even a small crew in the dead of night wouldn't be on high alert. The captain would keep one man on watch while the rest slept. After all, they were in port.

Despite all those thoughts, I didn't want to discourage her. We might not spot whoever placed the bomb on the yacht, but there might be something else we saw. If we could get our eyes on Dani's family, it meant we might track their movements.

I wondered again about reaching out to the CIA man, Smith. He'd have the resources we didn't. There was a problem with that. I'd make myself beholden to Smith and the CIA, something I had no desire to do.

The young server appeared with my beer and Dani's frozen drink. We ordered a plate of fish and shrimp tacos with a plate of ceviche to share. Hopefully it would make up for the order we ran out on back on Isla Mujeres.

"I'm going to the ladies' room," Dani announced.

I leaned back in my chair and sipped from the bottle. About six hundred yards offshore, a pair of gray dorsal fins popped up in the waves. The two dolphins disappeared under the surface, and I tracked north until I saw them reappear. I watched them continue along their path, vanishing under the water for a few seconds before cresting through the waves. They weren't in a hurry, and it seemed like they were just meandering around the island. After a bit, the dorsals disappeared for good, and I continued to watch the tops of the waves for any sign of them.

The server appeared with the ceviche, and I glanced around, looking for Dani. She hadn't returned from the bathroom, and I scooped a chip into the dish. As soon as the bite hit my stomach, I realized how hungry I'd been.

After three slow bites, I took another look around the open-air dining area. The couple around the firepit were working on another frozen cocktail. Two other couples occupied tables across the room.

"Is everything all right?" the server asked, appearing at my side.

"My friend might have gotten lost in the restroom," I remarked. My stomach knotted, but I tried to calm myself. She might just be taking some time. After all, the only bathroom she'd had for a couple of days was the one on *Carina*. That one would feel microscopic to most people.

"I can check," the girl volunteered. I thanked her and watched as she walked back toward the front of the restaurant. While I waited, I crunched another tortilla chip in my mouth.

It took only a couple of seconds for the server to return, and she shook her head as she approached.

"*Señor*, there is no one in the ladies' room," she informed me.

"Is there another one close by?" I questioned.

"In the lobby," she explained.

"I'll be right back," I promised her, rising to my feet and heading into the lobby. The restroom there was also empty, so I returned to the one in El Caribeño.

Pushing the door open, I saw nothing amiss. A wadded paper towel lay on the floor, but otherwise there was nothing unusual.

When I returned to the table, I found Dani still hadn't returned. Now, my instincts were firing off warnings. Where had she gone?

12

The ceviche lost its appeal, and I slunk into the chair. Two minutes ticked by as I considered what happened. There were too many entrances to the hotel she might have used for me to attempt any pursuit. Too much time had passed. Plus, it came down to whether she ran, or someone grabbed her.

The hotel was busy enough that grabbing her would be difficult. Far from impossible. The two goons from Isla Mujeres could approach her. If they carried weapons, and they did when they chased us off the island, they could force her to go along with them.

Or they could entice her with something else.

When the two first approached us in the diner, it seemed like they didn't want to cause immediate harm to Dani. If they only wanted her dead, it would have been easier to catch us coming out of the restaurant or on the street. Two bullets could end that problem right there.

They tried to shoot at you, dumbass.

Me, not Dani. They didn't pull their guns until I got in their way. Even when I was fleeing on *Carina,* Jack was firing at me while Dani was out of sight.

That didn't comfort me. I'd been wrong about situations like that before, and I didn't intend on letting Dani become a victim.

The waitress returned, looking worried. I handed her a hundred-dollar bill and asked, "Can I speak to your manager?"

Her eyes darted to the empty chair Dani had occupied, then she nodded. It took the manager, an American woman in her thirties, less than fifteen seconds to appear. She sported a linen pantsuit that implied a level of professionalism or, at least, what the hotel chain wanted to express. It had a casual business-like appearance—what guests in paradise expect from their hoteliers. From the concern on her face, the waitress had already briefed her on the situation.

"I'm Lisa, the restaurant manager," she greeted me, extending her hand.

"Lisa, my companion is missing," I explained, knowing that she already knew that. "I think it's possible someone took her."

She straightened her back. The fear of kidnapping remained a strong worry among most Americans. Even for someone like Lisa who lived full time in Mexico, the threat of being grabbed was a constant one.

Hotel staff see many things. I had in my brief career working at the Tilly Inn. Couples fight and split up, sometimes within a round of drinks. It's not unusual for one of a pair to storm off and disappear. However, the hotel doesn't want to skip its due diligence for fear that this time something more sinister happened.

"Would you like to contact the police?" she asked.

"Can we start with your hotel security?" I questioned. "I don't know why she would have just left, but if that's all it is, I don't want to cause too big of a scene."

"Why don't you follow me?" Lisa suggested.

I trailed behind her. Her crisp linen pants swooshed as she strode toward the lobby.

"Are you a guest with us today, Mr.—um, what was your name?"

"Gordon," I answered. "No, I'm not staying with you. We are staying on my sailboat, and we had just visited the marina here."

She paused at the front desk, where another woman a few years older than Lisa greeted her.

"Maria, can you call Stefan for me?" Lisa asked.

The woman behind the desk lifted the receiver and called. I scanned the lobby. There were six guests scattered around the room. Three sat at a small table to the side. Two were waiting on an elevator, and the last was standing about eight feet from me, where he leaned over the front desk and studied a map of the island. His finger traced along the roads as if he were searching out his desired route.

"Mr. Gordon, this is our security director," Lisa said to me, as she turned to regard a man approaching us. "Stefan, Mr. Gordon's companion has gone missing."

I turned my attention to the short, thick Latino man. He had a thin mustache that matched his thinning hair. His eyes narrowed when Lisa explained my situation.

"Do I need to call the police?" he asked, repeating Lisa's earlier inquiry.

My head tilted before I made an excuse to avoid that. "I'd like to make sure she didn't just leave," I told him. "She didn't indicate she was going to leave, but if that's all it is, I would hate to involve the authorities."

"Stefan can take care of you, Mr. Gordon," Lisa told me as she excused herself, washing her hands of the situation.

"What is your friend's name?" he asked.

I'd already considered the question while we waited for Stefan to arrive. How much information should I offer? It seemed like the answer to that was all. There was no reason to suspect anyone at the hotel was involved, however, that didn't rule it out just yet. After all, *Serendipity's Odyssey* floated at anchor only a few hundred yards from the hotel, just a few days before it exploded.

Still, if he suspected I held something back, it might make it more difficult. Besides, he held himself like a cop. The security guy at the Tilly Inn had been a former policeman, and he had some contacts in the force that helped move things along. Perhaps Stefan was in the same position.

"Danielle Traylor," I answered.

"Are you staying with us?" he asked.

"No, we were just here for lunch."

"And what happened?" Stefan inquired.

I gave him a synopsis: we ordered drinks and lunch, Dani went to the restroom, and she didn't return.

Stefan's brow furrowed. "You think she might have left on her own?"

"I don't think so, but she and I have only recently become acquainted."

This gave him a stern expression of concern.

"Do you have cameras covering the exits?" I asked.

"Yes, we have all the doors covered by surveillance."

"Can we just check and see if she left on her own?"

Stefan bit his bottom lip as he considered this.

"I'm not sure if you'll recognize her name," I added. "However, her father is Vincent Traylor of Traylor Technologies."

It was a gamble, but I guessed that if the Traylors had parked their yacht so near to the hotel, it might make a regular destination for them. After all, I doubted that Dani's father or sister cooked much for themselves.

Stefan's eyes widened some. "You know *Señor* Traylor?"

Bingo. Score one for me.

"We've talked before." It was only a half lie. It could have been Vincent Traylor on the other end of the radio.

"I thought *Señor* Traylor left?" Stefan remarked.

"He did," I replied. "His daughter didn't."

He nodded. "Let's look," he offered. "But if it appears as if *Señorita* Traylor was under duress, I'll alert the police."

"I expect nothing less," I told him, assuring him of my cooperation.

He led me to a room behind the front desk. It was a small office, only sixty square feet. A large computer monitor sat on a cheap metal desk. Stefan squeezed into the swivel chair, and I stood behind him.

"What time did you come into the hotel?" he asked.

I glanced at the clock on his desk. We'd been in the hotel for thirty-two minutes, but I had to remind myself what time zone that put me.

"Right at two," I answered, giving him a few extra minutes.

Stefan typed into the computer, and the computer monitor split into eight boxes showing different camera angles.

"We came in that door," I told him, pointing to the feed showing the entrance closest to the restaurant. The security man just nodded and allowed the playback to continue.

A counter on the bottom of the screen ticked seconds by and after forty-seven, Dani and I walked across the screen.

"Is this her?" he asked me.

"Yes," I confirmed.

We watched as the two of us walked into the restaurant and greeted the hostess. As we found our seats overlooking the sea, I watched the other feeds. Several people crossed the cameras as they entered the hotel. By the time the waitress was taking our drink order, I narrowed my gaze at a pair that came through the main entrance.

It was a man and a woman. The woman was unfamiliar to me, but while the camera didn't get a good angle on the man, I was sure it was the goon, Jack. He kept his head down, but I watched them as they came through the lobby.

On the other feed, I saw Dani get up from the table.

"She's leaving you here?" Stefan asked.

"Yes, she said she was going to the bathroom," I acknowledged.

"Mmm," he murmured to himself.

Dani entered the bathroom. Ten seconds later, the woman who entered with Jack followed her. I searched the other cameras for Jack, but he wasn't visible. My attention turned back to the door of the bathroom. Two minutes after Dani entered alone, she came out with the woman next to her.

I watched her walk past the front desk and outside with the woman. Then Jack strolled by the desk and left the hotel.

"Can you look outside?" I asked.

Stefan switched the screen to show the exterior. Lush green grass I'd seen outside earlier only looked gray on the black-and-white screen. Two women appeared in the frame. The new female was telling Dani something, and she nodded in response as the two approached a light-colored Nissan X-Trail.

Damned black-and-white screen.

Dani climbed into the back seat with the other woman. When Jack appeared, he got into the driver's seat and pulled away. I got a quick look at the license plate. KIH 32-43.

A round sticker on the back of the Nissan read, "AR." It was a logo of some sort.

"It seems she left on her own," Stefan pointed out.

I didn't think it was prudent to argue with him. She had appeared to go on her own, but given that Jack was there, I didn't think it was voluntary.

Stefan paused the video, freezing the Nissan X-Trail as it exited the driveway. He turned toward me with dispassionate eyes.

"Women sometimes are difficult," he offered as if it was some consolation to me. Although, I judged from his eyes that he assumed Dani made a getaway from me by finding a friendly face in the bathroom.

"Do you know what that means?" I asked, pointing at the "AR" on the back of the Nissan.

Stefan leaned over and turned off the monitor. "*Señor*, I think it would be smart to leave the girl alone."

I paused, realizing he now shifted me into the bad guy zone.

"You know what? You're right Stefan," I admitted to him. "I just met her, so there's nothing there. I just wanted to make sure she was safe."

The security chief nodded, but it wasn't in agreement.

"I'm sorry to waste your time," I told him.

"Would you like me to have the valet arrange you a cab, Mr. Gordon?" He put a heavy emphasis on my name, as if to remind me he knew who I was.

I shook my head. "No thanks, Stefan. I have a ride," I lied as I exited his office.

As I headed for the front door, I glanced back to see the man standing in the doorway of his office watching me leave. As soon as I was out of sight, I figured he'd call someone he knew in the local police to check on me.

I quickened my pace to the door, lifting the sunglasses up to shield my eyes. A Jeep Wrangler pulled past me into the valet parking. As I stepped back to give the driver room,

I noticed another sticker on the back of the Jeep. A round, red label with "AR" in the center. Around the rim, the words "*Autos se renta*" scrolled.

A car rental agency.

13

"I can't give you that information," the twenty-something Latino man stated.

The giant logo on the wall matched the one on the back of both the Jeep and the Nissan. A giant red ball. The sign offered a bit more information than the stickers had, reading "Cozumel's Auto Rental" in English and "*Autos Se Renta*" in Spanish.

His protestations weren't genuine, and as soon as he insisted that sharing that information was against the company's policy, I knew he'd bend the rules. Like anything done under the table, it came down to a matter of negotiation. His reticence persisted, but only because of mistrust. He might not want to lose his job over something like this, and an infraction like giving out customers' information would do that. If it didn't also get the kid in trouble with the law. In the US, privacy issues had become severe enough to warrant legislation.

"Listen," I said, noting his name tag that read Tomas. "Listen, Tomas, this is an urgent situation."

"Why didn't you call the police?" the boy asked in perfect English. The question was apt, and how I answered it might influence if he helped me.

"Do you think the police would help?" I asked.

He took a breath, surprised at the question. Or, at the least, taken off guard. "They are supposed to."

"The people who took my friend are planning to take her out of the country," I explained, not knowing if any of that was true. "Or worse."

At that point, prudence suggested I make my move, sliding a crisp hundred-dollar bill across the counter. That was more than he made in a week handing out keys to tourists. His eyes flicked from my face to the cash and back in a microsecond. His hand reached over and pulled the bill out of sight.

"Let me check," he offered as he glanced around. I wasn't sure if anyone else was in the office with us, but I guessed from his reaction there was a looming presence somewhere. By the time he turned to his computer, the hundred-dollar bill vanished into his pocket.

"The license number was KIH 32-43," I told him. "It was a Nissan X-Trail."

He typed the car plate into the computer. "It's a corporate rental. "

"What does that mean, Tomas?"

"A company rented it. TGH Inc."

My forehead wrinkled as my face scrunched. I would bet that was a fake name.

"Is there an address?"

"It's a PO box in California," Tomas answered.

"Of course it is," I sighed.

"I have a credit card number," he advised, shifting his eyes to me.

I waited, but Tomas stated, "I can't just give you that."

The kid was savvy for sure. I laid another bill on the counter and thought I was burning through my cruising kitty for this. Most of the time, I didn't spend a hundred bucks a week on anything.

Tomas snapped the cash up before printing the information on the computer screen. He grabbed it off the printer, folding it in half as he handed it to me.

"That's all I got on it."

"When did they say they would return it?" I asked.

He looked at the computer again. "They have it through Friday."

It was only Sunday. Were they planning to stay on the island that long? Or had they just booked it for a week without caring how long they kept it? After all, they could drop it after hours—if they returned it at all.

"Can I check back with you in case they return it early?"

He nodded. "Want me to call you if they do?" he suggested.

Shaking my head, I told him, "I don't have a phone."

Tomas shrugged, and I gave him a quick nod before leaving.

Outside, I unfolded the page to read the information. There wasn't much of use. A credit card number, a mailing address that led to a PO box, and a company name. The rental company didn't ask for a local address. There were only so many places on an island like Cozumel to take a car, so perhaps they didn't see it as a necessity. Of course, I'd make a terrible businessman because most things I saw companies do seemed ludicrous. Yet, those companies succeed, leading me to assume I just don't understand marketing.

A small red hatchback pulled up along the curb, coming to a stop in front of me. I took a step back, studying the car that I realized carried the VW logo on the grill. The passenger window rolled down.

"Gordon, get in," a voice shouted.

I bent over to peer into the little car. Andrew Smith sat behind the driver's wheel. He beckoned me into the passenger's side.

"Smith?" I questioned.

"Just get the fuck in the car," he demanded.

I opened the door and slid into the seat. "You could be more polite about it," I scolded him.

"Fuck you," he growled.

"You have such a sweet mouth," I commented. "I'm guessing you kiss your sister with that."

He cut his eyes to me as he shifted the Volkswagen into first gear and pulled into traffic.

"You lost the girl?" he questioned.

I turned my head to stare at him. "You've been keeping tabs?"

"I'm CIA," he remarked. "That's kind of our job."

"Smith, I'm a little tired to banter," I informed him. "Why don't you cut to the chase?"

"You're already working on this," Smith pointed out. "Why don't you start working with me?"

"I can think of a dozen reasons," I said. "Most start with trust. You're CIA, and I've yet to come across a spook that wouldn't burn an asset for their own skin."

"You don't have to trust me to work with me," Smith suggested.

"I appreciate you not giving me some spiel about learning to trust you," I noted.

"There's no point," he replied. "Who took the girl?"

I lifted the paper in my hand. "If I knew that, we wouldn't be talking."

"Who is she?" Smith asked.

My head cocked to evaluate the agent. "You don't know? That's your job."

"I can't get everything," he explained. "There's only me watching you from a distance."

"Since when?" I asked.

"Since when?" he repeated. "When what?"

"How long have you been watching me?"

"Since you showed up at the marina this afternoon," he told me. "It was the last place anyone saw Vincent Traylor."

"And you were staking it out?"

"Something like that. Here I am sitting in my car when, lo and behold, Chase Gordon shows up."

I shook my head in disbelief. "That was Traylor's daughter."

Smith furrowed his brow. "She was supposed to be on the boat with him."

"Not Carlee."

Realization dawned in his eyes. "The other daughter—Danielle? She's in London. As far as we know, she's had no contact with her family in years."

"Well, that's not the case. She and her sister have been talking. Now, Dani—Danielle wants to know what happened to her family."

Now Smith shook his head. "See, this is why I needed you helping me out. We did not know the sisters were talking."

"Why don't you tell me what your interest is? The CIA doesn't investigate murders, even if the victims manufacture weapons for the government. That means you want something else."

Smith didn't respond as he turned off the street on to a one-lane road heading east away from the port.

"Someone stole something. That's it?" I asked. "Plans for some weapon? Then the thieves killed the Traylors to cover it."

"Not plans," Smith answered.

I waited. The agent pulled off the road onto a scrubby lot. He slipped the Volkswagen into neutral and set the parking brake.

"It's too hot to turn off the air," he told me.

Smith shifted in his seat to face me. "Do you know anything about Vincent Traylor?" he asked me.

"Only what little I've learned about him from his daughter. He makes weapons and sells them."

"For a metric shit ton of money," Smith added. "The man is a billionaire, due to government contracts with the Department of Defense. He's also one of the largest contributors to the president."

"Makes sense," I considered. "Sure, makes it easy to be the guy selling to the US if he's got the president in his pocket."

"Don't kid yourself, Gordon," Smith remarked. "Every politician is in someone's pocket. A man from Idaho doesn't get into the Oval Office because he was honest and true. Those virtues don't pay the advertising rates on the public access channels, much less the major networks. Politics isn't about who is best for the job. It's about who can afford to be out there."

"Yeah, yeah, yeah," I groaned. "That's why I prefer to be out of the system."

"But you were a soldier," Smith reminded me.

"A Marine," I corrected him. "Hating the system our government has become is not the same as hating the country. I've fought for the US and seen my friends die for the same cause. Politics belittles that sacrifice."

"Fine," Smith conceded. "But someone killed the president's friend and supporter, rather spectacularly. That can draw certain eyes to the situation."

"Like the media?"

"Correct," Smith acknowledged.

"I'm guessing that the people who took Dani are the same that killed her father. Why?"

Smith shook his head. "I'm not sure. In fact, the only thing I know is what our inside agent gave us."

"You have someone in Traylor Tech?"

Smith nodded. "The information they gave us was that Traylor Technologies developed a small handheld missile."

"Like a Javelin?" I asked, referring to the anti-tank missiles.

"These are smaller," Smith explained. "If the information we have is correct, they pack a bigger punch."

"How much bigger?"

"Our source suggests that each Spike—the missile itself—contains a small nuke capable of decimating a city block."

"Wait, you said they didn't get the plans?"

Smith shook his head. "Traylor Tech made about thirty of these small spike nukes."

"And they're missing?"

"Technically, they never existed. There are no records showing they've been manufactured at any Traylor Tech facility."

I inhaled a sharp breath. "And your inside man couldn't confirm it?"

He shook his head again.

"How high up is he?" I questioned.

"Second in command."

"Wait," I exclaimed. "That's the daughter—Carlee."

Smith nodded.

"Shit!" I breathed.

14

"The agency could use your help on this," Smith admitted.

I shook my head. "Not a chance."

"Gordon, we're talking about a nuclear threat. Do you realize how easy it would be to walk across the border with a device the size of a telescope?"

I folded my arms. "You guys let him build them. Why don't you send an actual agent to stop him?"

"If this got out, do you realize the blowback the government, and the White House would receive if word leaked that one of the president's chief donors built thirty handheld nukes behind the country's back?"

"I imagine it would be bad," I agreed.

"We can't openly investigate the matter," Smith explained. "That would make the public relations on this even worse. The agency—no, the United States needs an independent operator to look into it."

"Not my problem, Smith," I replied.

"You can't ignore a threat like this."

"My only concern is finding Danielle."

"That's all part of it, Gordon," Smith retorted. "With Traylor and his other daughter dead, that puts your girl as the de facto head of the board."

"She works for an anti-nuke non-profit. I don't think she'd make a good leader for a weapons manufacturer."

"It won't matter," Smith said. "She's still going to be the key to getting any kind of semblance of leadership established before news of the Traylors' deaths break."

"You have no idea where these nukes are," I pointed out.

"But if Danielle Traylor takes control, she could help you find out whether or not they exist. Maybe we can get lucky, and this is only a play to manipulate the stock prices."

I lifted an eyebrow. Since a hollowed-out scuba cylinder held all of my financial security, any stock market or Wall Street lingo was nothing more than voodoo to me.

"The death of both a CEO and chairman of the Board will send the price of the stock into the cellar. It would make Traylor Technologies ripe for a hostile takeover. With no leadership in place, an acquisition like that would be easier."

"And if you get Dani in place, you can control that."

"Somewhat," Smith agreed. "It would be better if we knew that the head of one of the largest arms manufacturers was still friendly to our policies."

I nodded, not so much in agreement as understanding. If the company were to be taken over by a foreign or even adversarial company, they might shift sales of missiles to organizations that were anti-American or, in the best-case scenario, not in line with our allegiances. It led me to wonder how and why the government allowed independent contractors to build and sell weapons like that. However, like I said, when it came to the financial side of things, it was outside my scope.

"We can pay you," Smith added. "A significant amount."

"You can't afford it," I assured him. "Why doesn't the US buy the stock to prevent a takeover?"

"The US government doesn't operate corporations," Smith stated.

"Right," I snarled sarcastically. "And there are no sharks in the ocean. Don't feed me that bullshit."

"It's more complicated than that, though. The SEC would stop us, and even if we could avoid that, there'd be little way to contain the secret. Even if we used a shell company, the news of any takeover is going to hit the financial news. Since it's a prominent government contractor, CNN and Fox News will be all over it. That's scrutiny we don't want."

"That makes far more sense," I advised him. "If you want me to help you, feeding me crap isn't the way to do it. I get it is instinct for you to just spit out whatever lies you can, but I am not working that way."

"So, you'll help?" Smith questioned with a gleam of hope in his eyes.

"I need your help too, though."

Smith straightened up. "What?"

"My number one priority is finding Dani first. After that, we can work on your nukes."

He nodded. Whether or not it was begrudgingly, I
didn't know. His demeanor, though, was reticent, and I
still didn't trust him. But he offered me an opportunity to
trace the information Tomas had just given me.

"The kid at the car rental gave me a credit card. Can you
run it and get all the most recent charges?"

Smith nodded. "That's easy."

"How soon can you do it?"

"Couple of hours," he replied. "What are you looking
for? The card will belong to a fake company."

"It is," I assured him.

"Then that won't get you anywhere."

"The people who took Dani used a card to rent a car. It
would make sense for them to use the same card to pay for
a place to stay. I'd bet it's a house somewhere."

"What do you do when you find it?" Smith asked.

"I march inside and get Dani out."

"Assuming she's still alive," Smith suggested.

The thought already crossed my mind. If, as the agent
mused, someone killed the Traylors as an attempt to
sink the stock prices, then Dani was a liability. She
might already be dead. However, that thought didn't help
matters. I had to go on the assumption that she was still
alive and needed rescue. Until I found out otherwise, the
mission was to get her out.

Plus, I didn't like the idea of that. The murder of two
people just to lower the stock price seemed, well, to be
blunt, overkill.

"Remember, the goal is to find the nukes," Smith
reminded me.

I stared at him for several seconds without speaking.

"After we get the girl," he amended.

"Did Carlee give you any idea who was buying the missiles?" I asked.

Smith shook his head. "No, she thought her father was keeping it too close to the chest."

"So basically, you know nothing?" I questioned.

He shrugged.

"You really can't afford me," I repeated, more to myself than to the agent.

He grinned a cunning smile, saying, "I think we can."

15

The forty-five rotated in my grip after I'd put it
back together. Smith hadn't called me back with the
information from the credit card number. I didn't like
waiting, and during the last few hours, I'd cleaned my
service weapon and pulled out some dark clothes. It would
be dark in the next hour, and I hoped he would get me
some kind of lead.

If he came back with a hotel, my plans would have
to change. However, I bet that the people who took her
would want some privacy. The Marriott might frown on
holding people hostage in one of their suites, and there
were too many opportunities for Dani to be noticed by
hotel staff.

That made me think they would rent a house. If it were
me, I'd get one away from the tourist center of the island
too. One inland, without a lot of neighbors. That offered
them the protection they needed. I hoped that was their
thinking, because it also made it easier for me to craft and
attack without prying eyes. Privacy can work both ways.

I set the automatic to the side. It had a full magazine,
and I laid an extra one beside it. On the table in *Carina,*

I now had a Ka-Bar knife, the M45, a small bundle of zip ties, and a burner cell phone from Agent Smith.

There was an anxiousness flowing through me. It was a familiar sensation before any mission. Tonight, the feeling heightened because I didn't know what it would entail.

I'd hoped to have something before dark. The best approach would still be after dark, but at least a quick pass during the day would give me a better idea of what to expect.

I rose to my feet and moved into the galley. The cupboards were still bare since I hadn't had the chance to resupply in Isla Mujeres. I found a can of chicken and whipped up some chicken salad with the remnants of a mayonnaise jar and a handful of raisins and dried blueberries. Unfortunately, I didn't have any bread or crackers, so I ate the mixture with a spoon.

The phone vibrated across the table, and I grabbed it.

"I got an address," Smith told me before I could answer. He started rattling off a number as I scrambled for somewhere to write it down.

"Hold on," I scolded. "Repeat that."

Smith gave it to me again. The address was in El Cedral, a small village in the interior of the island. Pleased at my earlier deduction, I smiled at myself.

"When are you going?" he asked.

"As soon as I hang up with you," I replied.

"I can be there in ten minutes," he informed me. "Unless you rented a car this afternoon."

Unfortunately, I hadn't. My plan had been to get a taxi most of the way. When I left, I figured I'd take the rental car Jack was driving.

"No, I didn't," I said.

Smith didn't respond. Instead, the line went dead as he hung up on me. I scooped the rest of the chicken salad into my mouth and grabbed the M45 and other gear. I was wearing some black fatigues and boots, an unusual attire for me. Normally, I stick to a swimsuit or shorts and a t-shirt. My toes haven't been enclosed in months since mostly I wear either sandals or flip-flops.

But I guessed I might trek off the beaten path, and I wanted to be prepared.

The red hatchback wheeled around the corner, and I watched the car rock as Smith took the turn too quickly. A screech of tires sounded as he slammed the brakes. When it finished sliding to a stop, I opened the door and climbed into the passenger seat.

"Drive a little more conservatively when we approach the house," I suggested.

"It's only a four-cylinder," he complained. "Are you worried we'll get dragged into a race?"

"No, I'm concerned you're going to roll the car in a turn or just draw attention to us."

Smith rolled his eyes.

"I thought spies were supposed to be discreet," I commented.

"Have you seen the locals driving around here?" he inquired. "They don't even stop for the red lights and

RED LIGHT AT NIGHT

stop signs. I'm just trying not to stand out like your grandmother tooling along the country road to bingo."

"My grandmother didn't play bingo," I remarked.

Smith surveyed me before shifting the Volkswagen into gear. "You look like you're going on a jungle campaign," he quipped.

"The village is in the jungle," I pointed out. "This isn't just a stroll up to the house like the Welcome Wagon."

"What's your plan?" he asked.

"We do a quick drive-by," I explained. "I want to see what the house looks like. Are there trees around it? Lighting? That kind of thing."

"Do you expect any problems?"

"Yes," I answered, adding nothing further. Prudence suggests always expecting problems. Plan for the worst and hope for the best. More than one commander told me, in some form or fashion, hope isn't a strategy.

Tonight, I wouldn't have the luxury of an in-depth plan. We were striking on the fly. I had one or two passes to get a feel for the house. While Smith drove, I pulled up the map on the burner phone. The image showed the address as one of three houses on a short residential street.

El Cedral was more like a clearing in the center of nothing but trees. The house we were going to backed up to acres of greenery on the map. If the vegetation was like most of the island, it would be four-to-six-feet-tall scrub brush.

The best approach would be from the rear through that brush. I studied the house. With no plans, I'd have to rely on what I considered common sense architecture.

Most homes here carried similar features. The aerial view
of this one showed a pool behind the house. That often
meant entering the pool and patio area would lead into the
main living area. The kitchen should connect to that, and
judging from the shape, I guessed it was in the front corner.
That would leave at least a master bedroom on the ground
floor and two or three rooms on the second level.

If I could come through the kitchen, there'd be less
chance of someone being in that room. Especially since I
planned to wait until after midnight to enter the house.

I turned off the phone. It was the best plan I had until I
saw the house itself.

That took about thirty more minutes. During that time,
Smith tried to start a conversation, but I wasn't responsive.
He and I didn't have the rapport to joke before a mission.
Instead, I needed to focus on what I was about to do.

When we reached El Cedral, Smith cruised the streets
of the little village. I wanted to see what was on the
neighboring streets. If a police station sat a block away,
then there might be a quick response to any gunfire.
Luckily, the only thing in the vicinity were three different
bars and two restaurants.

Overall, the community struck me as an upscale one.
There were likely more than a few vacation rentals in the
mix, but many of the homes showed regular life.

When we passed our target house, I examined the
exterior. Even in the dark, I could make out the white
stucco and red ceramic roof tiles. A four-foot perimeter
fence constructed of concrete and wrought-iron rails
surrounded the villa.

"Keep going," I ordered Smith.

"Any problems?" he asked again.

I shook my head. The place looked quiet. If my estimations were close, there were only a few people in the house with Dani. If she was even there, I reminded myself.

"Pull over here," I told him when we reached a small stretch of road with only a couple of dark houses nearby.

"What do you want me to do?" he asked.

"It's going to take me at least a couple of hours," I explained. "I don't want to breach the house until late. Find someplace out of the way and wait."

Smith nodded.

"If I'm not back by dawn—well, it's probably bad."

"Then make it back," he replied.

"Aww, shit, Smith. It's almost like you care." Before he could respond, I bounded out of the door and vanished into the shadows between the empty houses.

There was no moon out, and Cozumel had few streetlights, leaving me shuffling through the night. It took about five minutes for my eyes to adjust. By then, I was already behind the residences and into the scrubs. The branches scraped over my skin, and after kicking at least two sizable stones, I knew that opting for the boots over the flip-flops was wise.

I needed to head north for a quarter of a mile before I turned back to the east. There was no one out, and I didn't need to worry about staying out of sight. The closest house was three hundred yards away, and in the night, I was invisible. As long as I didn't break out any wolf howls, nothing would detect me.

Once I made my final approach to my target, I'd slow my pace, ensuring I made deliberate and silent movements.

Something moved in the bushes, and I paused, giving whatever animal it was plenty of time to move away from me. Most animals, even dangerous ones, wanted to get away far more than they wanted to attack. Anything out in the night with me would have more fear of me, and I'd let it scamper, slither, or scurry away without harm.

Half an hour after I exited the Volkswagen, I stared down from a slight rise in the landscape at the white and red villa. Lights shone from the windows onto the patio. The pool, however, was dark.

I watched for several minutes until a figure exited a sliding glass door and stepped out by the pool. Only the lights from the house illuminated the patio, and when the man lighted a cigarette, I could see the flicker of flame from his lighter. In a few seconds, the air filled with the acrid smell of tobacco.

It wasn't Jack or Hammer, but the figure belonged to a tall man, somewhere around six foot five. He didn't appear armed. Or, at least, if he was, it was a small handgun tucked away. There was no holster on his side, and he wore a t-shirt that didn't hide a shoulder holster.

No one was expecting trouble, and if he was actually on guard duty, it was lax. I'd have no trouble creeping up behind him. After three minutes, the man flicked the cigarette across the concrete before returning to the house.

After lowering myself down on my haunches, I waited. An hour passed, and there was no more sign of life from the house. My internal clock told me it was almost eleven.

The sliding door squealed again as the same figure appeared by the pool. Flame ignited again as he lit another cigarette. He paced along the pool this time. After three circuits around the water, he tossed his cigarette again and headed back inside. The light streaming through the glass doors blinked out.

At half past midnight, I hadn't seen another light come on. No one else came back outside. The occupants settled in for the night even if they weren't asleep.

It was time to go inside.

16

The best time to breach any structure was early
in the morning. When I led teams in attacking a
hostile stronghold, whether it was a house or a cave in
Afghanistan, I preferred the hours between three and four
in the morning. Most of the opposition was not just asleep,
but deep asleep. Any guards on duty had been on alert for
several hours, and they'd grown lax and tired.

I didn't want to wait that long.

As I straightened my legs, I stretched to unkink the
muscles that tightened while I waited. The M45 came out
of my waistband. I didn't wear a holster for it normally.
Most of the time, I left it on *Carina* since I was in a foreign
country. With it in my grip, I moved toward the house.

At the perimeter fence, I crouched and peered over the
concrete wall. No one moved inside. My legs remained
bent as I inched around the outside of the fence. There
was no entrance on the side where I thought the kitchen
might be. That only left the front door and the rear one by
the pool. I could jimmy the latch on the sliding glass door
easier.

Thirty seconds ticked by in my head before I moved. My left hand reached up and grasped the top of the ornate ironworks atop the fence. I heaved myself up and rolled over the top, landing in a squat. I waited motionless for several seconds. Nothing happened, and I moved toward the rear of the house.

When the smoker came out earlier, his movement didn't trigger any motion-sensor-controlled lights. I hoped they just didn't exist and that he hadn't turned them off. After the dash to the house, I was certain there weren't any.

My head extended around the corner to survey the patio. Clear.

When I reached the sliding door, I tested it. The smoker was smart enough to lock it, and when I pushed it to open it, the glass didn't budge.

The M45 slipped under my waistband as I removed the Ka-Bar. I pushed the door to open it, letting a small crack appear between the metal frame and the doorjamb before the latch prevented it from opening wider. The blade of the knife slipped into the crack, and I made a swift upward motion. There was an audible click as the metal of the Ka-Bar blade snapped the latch up. With a soft whoosh, the door slid open.

After a few seconds of continued silence, I stepped into the house, having re-sheathed the knife and drawn the forty-five. The barrel of the gun swept over the room, a large living space with a couch and two matching chairs. White, utilitarian ceramic tile covered the floor. As I moved into the house, I left the door open and took careful steps.

There was a rhythm to a house at night when everyone was asleep. It was a quiet that almost had a slow wheeze through it. I was certain that everyone was asleep.

My eyes scanned the room. The kitchen was in the corner, as expected, separated from the sitting room by a bar with shutters that could close it off from the rest of the house. With the shutters opened, I could see the glow of a clock on the microwave. The eerie green numbers cast the only light in the room, and I turned away from it. Across the room, an opening led to a darkened corridor.

The house made a cracking noise that landed somewhere between a bump and a creak. I froze in place, trying to judge from which distance the sound traveled. There was nothing but the stillness of the night.

Houses make noises all the time—often the result of external forces like wind or temperature. Perhaps even a mouse scampering through the walls caused an odd noise.

This wasn't a small rodent. The sound echoed through the downstairs, and I wondered how a noise that loud didn't wake up the neighbors.

There wasn't another noise, and I shuffled toward the steps, expecting someone to come from upstairs. By the time I realized no one was on the stairs, Jack appeared like a brutish wraith from the hallway. In the dark, he paused, confused at my presence.

"Wha—"

Before he finished the startled exclamation, I tried to take the four or five steps back toward him. The gap was too large, and he recovered his senses in time to throw up a defense for the blunt topside of the M45 I swung at him.

My intent was to drop him without firing the weapon, but the actual action failed.

His forearm came up, catching my wrist. The brawny man reacted again, outmaneuvering me as his other hand caught by the wrist. He jerked me forward, striking me in the face with his forehead—a move I often used myself to stun my opponent. It worked the way I would have intended it. On reflex, my body went limp for a split second. While I recovered, wrenching away before he could strike again, he dislodged the automatic from my grip. The sound of metal striking a marble floor resonated through the house.

Disarmed, I needed to get the advantage back, as if I ever had it in this match. My left foot kicked the forty-five away from both of us. If he didn't have a gun on him—for the first time, I realized he was wearing running shorts and a tank top—I didn't want him to get to it before I could.

In the dark, I didn't see where the gun went, and I ignored it, bringing my right foot around for a hook kick that caught him just below the solar plexus. The result wasn't as effective as I'd hoped. He floundered when my heel knocked him off balance.

I let my right foot land on the marble floor, using the momentum of the kick to bring my body around 180 degrees. My left foot, carried by the inertia of the spin, came out of the chamber and hit Jack on the side of the head.

The man twisted, losing what little footing he had after the initial hook kick. He tumbled over a sofa, knocking a lamp off the glass side table with a loud crash.

A door behind me slammed open, and I dove across the room as footsteps charged down the stairs. I slid across the marble floor, searching for the M45 as Hammer lumbered down the stairs. I chanced a glance over my shoulder to see the large man realize I was the one who incapacitated him with only a beer bottle the other day. Rage filled his face, and he launched off the landing at me.

As he dropped toward me, I rolled to the side, getting out of his path as he came at me. The grunt recovered faster than I'd hoped, landing in a crouch to launch another attack at me. This time, he hit me like a defensive tackle for the NFL. His shoulder drove me across the living room before smacking me against the solid stucco wall.

My right elbow wrapped around the man's neck, and I pulled him down as I fell to the floor. If I was going to go, I had every intention of taking him down with me. Gravity helped me out, and the pair of us crashed to the floor. He struggled to pull away from me, and when he could not, the big man pushed himself to his legs and twisted around in a whipping motion. My feet came off the ground as he hurled me around. I let go of his neck, allowing myself to tumble across the floor, out of his reach. As soon as I stopped moving, I scrambled across the floor.

A bare foot caught me in the chest, lifting me up as I grunted. Jack, now recovered from my kicks to him and with new vigor, came after me again. The second kick sent me to the side, and moving out of the way of the third allowed me to catch his calf and pull him off balance.

There was a sickening thud as the goon came down on his back. I crab crawled back to see his oddly misshapen form in the dark. His head cocked at an awkward angle from his body. A dark blotch puddled around his head.

"Arrgghh!" Hammer bellowed as he charged at me. I slid out of his grasp, and the brute tripped over his dead partner's legs in the dark. As he face-planted, I turned to search for the forty-five. The distinctive shape of the grip protruded from behind a large potted plant. Its dark shape contrasted against the white marble. I swooped over, scooped it up, and turned as Hammer pushed up off the floor.

The gun barked in the night, and Hammer flopped forward as the bullet blew through his skull. Footsteps ran across the floor above me, and I rotated on my right foot as a figure appeared on the steps. I counted two beats of my heart—long enough to determine it wasn't Dani—before I squeezed the trigger again. The newcomer almost stopped in his tracks as the forty-five-caliber round penetrated his rib cage and pulverized his heart. However, the bullet only paused him on the step for a microsecond before he rolled forward. His legs no longer carried him, but gravity and inertia kept him going forward into an off-kilter somersault down the steps. Sprawled on the landing, the man's body twitched as the last vestige of his nervous system ceased to function.

The forty-five extended in my hand toward the stairs. I waited in silence, allowing seconds to tick away on the timer in my head.

No one else came from upstairs. The house grew even more eerily quiet now that the dead occupied it. It was a creepy silence that came in the aftermath of death. I didn't let it fool me into thinking I was alone. My guard remained high as I stepped down the hallway.

In the darkness, a flash exploded with a boom. I fired twice into the dark. A clatter sounded, and I stepped forward. My foot nudged something, and I ran my hand along the wall until I touched the light switch. A skinny kid sprawled across the floor. He didn't appear to be out of his teens. A twenty-two revolver lay on the tile floor. I knelt down and picked it up. The gun was a piece of shit that no one cleaned in years. The snub-nosed barrel still emanated heat.

I shook my head. The stupid kid took a wild pop shot in the dark, and it cost him his life. Part of me felt guilt. This boy might have been Jack or Hammer's son. Or maybe he was a fresh recruit. I almost considered him innocent. He'd tied himself to the wrong people. That might not have been his fault.

On the other hand, he took the shot. At nineteen, I killed my first enemy soldier. That was another kid about the same age as I had been. His face still lingered in my head late at night. This kid's might not. After all, I've learned a lot about consequences. That nineteen-year-old Iraqi had far less choice than this one.

I put the twenty-two in my back pocket. It wasn't much good unless I was on top of someone, but it didn't take up much space either.

A muffled thump spun me around, and the M45 popped up in my grip. I moved into the kitchen where I'd heard the noise. The room was empty.

With a deep breath held in my chest, I listened. Now the house was silent. Or mostly, at least.

I reached for a large wooden door in the corner. Locked. Another muffled sound came from the other side.

"Dani?" I asked in a raised voice to penetrate through the wood.

"Mmm-mmm-mm," came the response.

The door opened out, and I'd have a hard time kicking it in past the jamb. "Stay back," I warned as I leveled the barrel of the automatic at the knob. I turned to angle the weapon into the frame.

As I turned my face away, I lifted my other arm to shield my head. The danger in shooting off a lock was shrapnel. At least for me. Wood and metal bits exploded outward. The person on the other side of the door had to worry about the bullet.

The handle shattered when I pulled the trigger. With the butt of the gun, I knocked the broken bits loose, letting them fall to the floor. The door opened an inch, and I raised the barrel up in case it was a trap.

Along the walls were rows of wine bottles resting, upturned in nooks, with their necks pointing downward. In the corner, a mass moved in the dark. I turned on the light to see Dani, tied on the floor with her hands and feet bound like a pig for slaughter. A cloth covered her face with a sash wrapped around her mouth like a gag.

I dropped to my knees and pulled the cloth off her face. She stared back at me, gasping for a breath of air.

17

"Are you hurt?" I asked her.

She shook her head. "Not really," Dani replied. "I was in here for hours, though."

"What happened?" I questioned.

"This woman surprised me in the bathroom," she explained. "She was with the guy that chased us from Isla Mujeres."

"I saw him," I told her.

"You did?" she responded with some surprise.

"On video," I explained. "After you disappeared, I found you on the surveillance."

"They threatened to kill me," she said.

"They can't hurt you now," I assured her. "What did they want?"

"The woman was asking me all these questions," Dani told me. "They thought Carlee told me something."

I cut the zip ties, binding her arms and legs. "Carlee wasn't just talking to you," I told her.

"What do you mean?" she asked as she rolled to her side, stretching her legs out and rotating her arms now that they were free.

"She was an informant for the CIA."

"Were these people with the CIA?"

I shook my head as I helped Dani to her feet. "What did she ask?"

"The woman," Dani replied. "She just kept asking me questions. About some code."

"Code?" I inquired.

Dani nodded. "Yeah. I heard her talking to that big guy. There's some warehouse in Merida."

"Your father's warehouse?"

"Yeah, she kept asking about dates and phone numbers."

"For the code?" I clarified.

Dani nodded.

"Did the woman say anything about your father's boat?" I asked. "Was she behind the explosion?"

Dani gave me a blank stare and a shrug.

"We need to get out of here," I stated, grabbing her by the arm. "I didn't see the woman here."

When we stepped into the hallway, Dani froze at the sight of the dead boy. The pause was only a second, and she turned away from the corpse. The woman took in the sight with only a couple of blinks of her eyelids. Not that she didn't register it. In fact, I felt the tension in the air as she took in an inhalation of air.

She was in a space between survival mode and relief. The up and down of adrenaline over the last couple of days numbed her senses. It was common, and it was the same reason this kid would occupy far less time in my brain than that nineteen-year-old Iraqi.

"Come on," I urged. "We have to move."

Dani didn't, though. Instead, some angry curiosity took hold. She stalked into the other room to see the bodies of Jack and Hammer.

"She's not here," Dani remarked.

I shook my head. "No woman," I confirmed.

"Where is she?" Dani demanded. Her voice raised an octave.

"We'll find her."

Dani turned to stare at me. "What did she want?" she questioned. "I mean with the codes."

"Let's go, I'll explain what I can," I offered as I reached out and pulled her along.

Instead of walking, she pressed up against me. Her arms tightened around my back as she pulled into my chest. I put my hands around her as well.

"What the hell, Chase?" she murmured into my chest.

"Your father might have made some missiles for them."

"Who are they?" she asked.

"Don't know yet," I admitted.

Dani pushed away from me. "We have to stop them," she insisted. "That woman was crazy."

"Crazy?" I repeated.

"Not like insane," Dani explained. "At least, not like out of her mind. More like she was on a mission."

I took her by the arm and guided her toward the door I'd come through. "We have a ride waiting on us," I said. "Let's get to the car and talk it out."

She nodded.

"Why do you continue to help me?" she wondered aloud.

"Maybe I like you," I pointed out.

"We've only known each other a couple of days," she reminded me.

I shrugged as we stepped into the night. It took several minutes to navigate through the brush to the road. When we reached Smith's car, I opened the back door for Dani.

Smith turned around in the driver's seat to stare at Dani. He shifted his gaze to me. "No problems?" he asked.

I didn't respond. Instead, I introduced Dani. "This is Andrew Smith, Special Spook to the CIA."

Smith extended his hand to Dani. "Glad to meet you."

She took his hand without squeezing it. "Thank you," she replied in a shaky voice.

Smith retracted his hand. "What did they want with you?" he asked her.

"Dani needs a quick update," I interrupted him.

"Damn straight she does," Dani snapped. "Chase said Carlee was your agent?"

"Not an agent," Smith explained. "She was a source—an informant."

"On my father?"

Smith nodded. "Among other things."

"Tell it all to her," I urged him.

Dani folded her arms across her chest and waited.

"The gist of it is that your sister informed us that Traylor Tech manufactured some nuclear missiles off the books. It's assumed they were for a foreign agency."

"Another country?" she asked.

"Or organization," he suggested. "But we don't know for sure where they might be or even if they exist."

"We might now," I offered.

"What did you learn?" Smith demanded.

"They grilled her for codes to a warehouse in Merida."

"Mexico?" Smith asked.

Dani shrugged. "I just heard Merida."

"That's pretty close to here," I reminded Smith.

"Traylor has a facility there," Smith explained. "It's a drone manufacturing plant."

"Guess they added nukes to the list," I suggested.

"What code did they want?" Smith asked.

Dani shook her head. "I don't know. It was numbers. She kept asking me for different dates. I only overheard her talking to someone outside about Merida."

"You think they got the numbers, though, right?" I clarified.

She nodded.

"Why would they need them?" Smith wondered.

"Any shipment had to have my father's approval before the warehouse released it. It used to be a thumb print, or if it was over the phone, it might be a coded phrase. Something that only he would have."

"We need to get to Merida," Smith stated.

"Now, wait," I interjected. "We got Dani back. That was all I needed to do. You have the details. Send in an armed response."

"To do what?" Smith inquired. "Raid a government contractor? Am I sending in some of your Marine buddies to shoot up innocent factory workers? In a plant that we know manufactures drones for the United States? That would look real good."

"We have to go," Dani remarked.

"What?" I asked.

"My father was an asshole all my life. He deserved to die, and in fact, I think blowing up in the middle of the ocean was too good for him. He made a bunch of nukes and planned to sell them to that bitch."

"We don't know that," I reminded her. "She might have killed him because he wouldn't sell them."

"I'd bet he just wanted more money," Dani scoffed.

"Who was the woman?" Smith asked.

"She didn't give me her name. She was in her forties. White with red hair. Bright red hair."

"That should stand out," Smith noted. "Gordon, you didn't mention the hair."

"I saw her on a black-and-white video," I reminded him.

The agent nodded with some annoyance.

"Chase, I've got to get to that plant," Dani admitted. "If I can stop them from delivering the missiles, that's something."

I glanced between her and Smith. The spook said, "She'd be the only heir to the business."

"Assuming her father left her in the will," I pointed out.

"By the time anyone realizes one way or the other, it will be too late," Smith pointed out.

With a sigh, I remarked, "I guess we're going to the mainland."

"You'll need a plane," Smith offered.

18

The Cessna buzzed through the air, and I let my head lean back in the rear seat. Dani leaned against my shoulder. Her steady breathing suggested she was sleeping. I didn't move during the hour after we'd taken off. The pilot, someone Smith arranged to fly us from Cozumel to Merida, hadn't spoken since takeoff. Smith only hired the man to fly. That was fine with me. I didn't feel like small talk, and Dani needed to rest.

We knew little information, but Smith promised he'd get a layout of the plant. For now, all I'd been able to do was study a satellite map on the internet. Traylor Tech's building was at the end of a road off Highway 180, the main road heading east out of Merida.

The city in Mexico was less than an hour south of Progreso, a popular coastal pueblo and port city. It had been nothing more than a fishing village for years until the local government funded a large pier. Now that it was getting more traffic, the town's business sectors grew. However, since the coast had few inlets or coves, it wasn't ideal for anchoring out.

The cabin was dark except for the glow of the instruments in the cockpit. I let the satellite image I'd studied earlier stretch out in my head. There appeared to be a fence stretching around the perimeter. There was only one entrance to the plant with a guard shack monitoring all traffic. From the shack, there was a drive that wound around the building to a loading dock. Another path led to the parking lot and main entrance.

If I were going to slip in unnoticed, I'd focus my attention on the southeast corner closest to the guard shack. It was just out of view of the security staff monitoring the gate, but it would be close enough that the guards wouldn't pay it much attention, thinking its proximity to the shack was protection enough.

However, we would not sneak in. I had the heir to the empire with me, and she and Smith both thought it would be easy to just waltz through the front doors with the Traylor name. Even if that worked, I wanted to form an idea for an escape plan. Should the shit hit the fan inside, we might have to make a hasty escape. Thinking out the routes made me feel better.

"Landing in five minutes," the pilot announced.

"Thanks," I told him as I checked my seatbelt. Dani continued to sleep, and I figured another five minutes would not hurt her.

It didn't take her that long to wake up. As the plane's pitch changed, she sat up, shaking herself awake.

"Are we there?"

The lights of the runway stretched out in the dark. I gestured my head toward them. The glowing path grew larger, and I leaned back. A minute later, the wheels squealed as they touched down. The Cessna bounced as the pilot decelerated.

"What's the plan?" she asked me as the plane slowed to taxi toward the hangar.

"Smith is supposed to have a car here for us," I told her. "We can take a couple of minutes to put ourselves together before heading to the plant."

"I'm a little nervous," she admitted. "It's stupid. My father always had that effect on me. The fucker."

I nodded in understanding.

"He's dead," I reminded her.

"Yeah, I know," she confessed. "But it's more than that. He's still a part of this company."

"You think it will remind you of him?" I asked.

She shook her head. "It will remind me of Carlee."

"Oh," I replied.

"I left her with him," she said.

"That's not on you, Dani," I assured her.

"But it is," she denied. "I should have gone back for her. Instead, I buried my head in London and forgot her."

"Nothing stopped her from leaving of her own accord."

"Could she?" Dani asked.

I didn't answer. She lost her sister, and there were no words to assuage her feelings. When my brother died, I thought it was my fault too. If I'd have stood up to my father, he might have given me the beating he did for David. I was bigger, and I could have taken it.

But none of that was true.

The only person who was at fault was my father. Even though I blamed my mother too, I knew in my gut that there wasn't much she could do either. She was a young woman with only a high school diploma in small-town Arkansas where little girls were expected to marry and have kids. There was no obvious escape for her. She didn't see a way out with three kids. That didn't excuse her for ignoring the fact that her husband murdered her son. For that, I don't forgive her.

I sighed. Emotions are hard.

"Smith told me to wait here," the pilot informed me, breaking my thoughts up.

We climbed out of the Cessna, stepping on the rough asphalt of the tarmac. A man stood next to a red Mustang convertible. He gave me a wave, and I approached.

"Are you Chase Gordon?" he asked.

I nodded, and he handed me a key fob. "Courtesy of Mr. Smith," he acknowledged.

"A little flashy," I remarked.

"This was what the rental company had available on a half-hour notice."

"I'll try not to scratch it," I promised him.

"Couldn't care less," he joked. "He told me to get the full coverage."

I chuckled as I opened the driver's door. Dani slid into the seat next to me. The Mustang was a newer model with the push start button. It barely made a sound as the engine turned over to life.

"This will work," I considered. "If we're going to pass you off as the head of the company, it will look best if you come in all flashy."

We followed 180 into the night. When I spotted the turnoff, I took the curve faster than I intended. Once we had gotten outside of the main metropolitan area, the streetlights vanished and the highway was pitch black. Only the glow of my headlights against the black canvas appeared.

Once we turned on the side street, I slowed down. A single halogen light illuminated a small building to the right. I could make out the shadows and silhouettes of large mounds. It would be the concrete plant I'd seen on the map. It meant we were two miles from the Traylor Tech plant, and in the distance, the night sky almost glowed from the lights.

I pulled off the road and slipped the M45 out. The plan was to stroll into the plant, but if we had any problems, I wanted to be prepared.

"Remember," I told Dani, "you're doing all the talking. I'm just the dumb bodyguard."

She nodded as I let my foot off the clutch and pulled back onto the potholed road.

Two minutes later, the large chain-link fence came into view. The building was an oasis of light, something I guessed from the glow it gave off miles away. As we pulled up, it felt like driving into the midafternoon sun from a tunnel. I blinked a few times, allowing my eyes to adjust.

"¿Puedo ayudarles?" the guard asked.

"Do you speak English?" Dani asked.

"Yes," he responded.

"I'm Danielle Traylor. I need to speak to whoever is in charge."

The guard wrinkled his nose as the name rolled around in his head. "Traylor, like the company?"

"Exactly like that," she snapped. "I'm your boss."

"Uh, I'll need to see some identification," he stammered, and I realized he was likely American, or at least English was his first language. Not that I could determine much in Spanish, but his diction was perfect in English.

Dani handed the man her passport, and he scrutinized it in the light glowing from the guard shack. I scanned the driveway between us and the main entrance. There were at least twenty cars parked around the lot. Most were newer, and an indication that Traylor paid well enough.

The fence had yellow warning signs in Spanish with a lightning bolt through a stick figure of a man—electrified. Not a surprise, since they were manufacturing weapons of mass destruction inside. However, what I'd seen so far could all be circumvented, and in my mind, I took notes.

The grounds were pristine and judging from the construction of both the building and the fences; it was all a new build. Even the landscaping was just now showing fresh growth, indicating the facility wasn't more than a couple of years old.

"I need to call my boss," the man told her.

"Hurry it along," Dani demanded. "I don't have all night. We're already late because of the plane."

The guard nodded and stepped back into the booth.

"Nice touch," I noted.

"I try," she admitted. "What are we looking for?"

"If we see your new friend, we start with her," I suggested. "Otherwise, we try to find out if they have a shipment of missiles waiting for delivery.

The guard had the phone cradled between his ear and shoulder. With every glance he cast out the window at us, I felt nervous. My index finger caressed the barrel of the forty-five wedged under my waistband.

I didn't want to end up in a shootout with the guards. After all, these guys were just doing their job, and as far as they knew, it was legitimate. That made them collateral damage, something I wanted to avoid at all costs.

If the security staff thought they were protecting not only the company they worked for but also securing US armaments, they'd react in a manner to do just that. We wouldn't get the same consideration. Instead, the guards would mete out deadly force to stop us.

Each breath I took was a concentrated one as I remained focused on the moment. The man in the booth continued to talk on the phone, but so far, no alarms seemed to have sounded in the plant.

After a minute, he hung up and opened the door to the shack.

"Ms. Traylor, Thomas Caplan, our head of security, is on his way here to meet you."

"He needs to hurry," Dani stated, lowering her voice an octave. I wanted to tell her to pull back on that. Even as the boss, there's a certain level of cooperation achievable through a softer approach.

"He is," the guard assured her.

"Good," she remarked.

19

"How long is this going to take?" Dani asked.

"I'm sorry, Ms. Traylor. He should be here any minute," the guard told her.

"Don't push it too much," I suggested.

"I know, but don't you think he'd get suspicious if I was waiting too patiently?"

I shrugged.

Headlights swept up behind us as a Land Rover pulled up, blocking me from backing up. Again, I touched the cold steel of the M45 and sucked in a breath.

"Ms. Traylor?"

"Yes," Dani replied, staring up at the man in his fifties standing next to the Mustang.

"I'm Thomas Caplan, head of security here. I've spoken with Mr. Donaldson, our chief of operations. He was unaware of any visit."

"Mr. Caplan, where is Donaldson?" she demanded.

"He's in DC right now."

"I think we should take our conversation somewhere a little more discreet," she insisted, throwing a wary glance at the guard shack.

Caplan scanned the area with some confusion.

"I guess, I mean, why don't you take us to your office?" Dani rephrased the sentence, adding some emphasis to the request. The shift in tone was impressive, and Caplan remained at a loss. It took him two or three seconds to nod in agreement.

"Why don't you just pull up to the front?" he suggested.

Dani motioned for me to drive, and I gave the guard a hard stare. He raised the gate arm that blocked our progress. I drove away before Caplan could get back into his Land Rover.

"So far, so good," Dani quipped, her voice lilting lightheartedly.

"I think your next roadblock is this Donaldson," I pointed out.

"Yeah," she mused.

"Have you given this any real thought?" I asked as I drove toward the lot.

"What do you mean?"

"You could really take this company over," I explained. "I'm not sure what your father's estate looked like, but if you are the sole heir, then it means you have to consider those things."

Her face changed. The intrigue of talking her way into a plant switched to trepidation. There was a reality to face, and so far, the rush of life-and-death danger had pushed that to the back of her mind.

"I could shut it down," she said without thinking.

"You could," I admitted. "But give it some thought."

"Why should I?" she asked. "We're making weapons that kill."

"Listen, I'm just a Marine," I told her. "So, what do I know? I don't enjoy killing any more than you do, but sometimes it's needed. And sometimes it's not the killing itself that's required, it's the threat of it."

"I get it, but look where we are. My father is—was—making missiles for terrorists."

"Then do better."

She curled her lip at me. "You're something," she stated.

I smiled at her and wagged my eyebrows. "Just wait and see," I quipped.

"Let's save the world first," she suggested, opening the door as Caplan's Land Rover pulled into the parking space next to us.

"Ms. Traylor, you aren't on the board," he stated without expression.

"I'm guessing you don't watch the news," Dani replied.

"What do you mean?"

"My father and sister were both killed earlier this week. There hasn't been a public statement by the company yet, but I can most assuredly tell you I'm now the only person you need to be concerned with."

"Uh," Caplan muttered. "Why don't we go up to my office?"

"I believe that is what I suggested doing," she reminded him. "While it's still your office."

Caplan led us through the glass doors into a small lobby. Customers didn't wander in off the street, but Traylor Tech did want to offer a modest reception area for auditors or inspectors coming on the behalf of both the government and Traylor Tech's clientele. An empty receptionist's desk stared back at the doors. The company decorated the space with art I didn't recognize but might either be a famous painter or another piece from a hotel auction. Four leather chairs sat on opposite sides of the room, dividing the room into matching quarters. While the lighting appeared to be a modern chandelier which had six bars intersecting at abstract angles, it still illuminated the lobby with intense brightness, an effect aided by the white marble floor.

We passed through a security checkpoint where another guard gave Caplan a nod as he swiped a magnetic card through the reader. As we walked by, I inspected the security man. He carried a Beretta nine-millimeter strapped to his right hip and wore a tactical vest. As I surveyed him, we locked eyes. The man was giving me the same treatment, and I lifted an eyebrow.

Caplan continued down the hall and opened a door. We stepped into his office, a modest space with a few pictures on the wall. The most notable one was a group of Rangers with their arms wrapped around each other. A much younger version of Thomas Caplan stared back at me. The backdrop of the picture was in Kuwait during Desert Storm. Caplan had aged, and like most of us, time had taken a toll. But the man didn't appear like he'd skipped all his PT since getting out of the Army. He might not keep up the same regime, but from the looks of him, he at least maintained a gym membership somewhere.

Dani seemed to be settling into the role of being in charge, and she dropped into the chair opposite the security chief's desk. I opted to remain standing.

"Mr. Caplan, I understand the concern you and Mr. Donaldson have," she started. "However, we, as a company, have a bigger problem right now."

"Ms. Traylor, I hadn't heard about your father," he told her. "I'm sorry."

Dani nodded without a thought. "Right now, sympathies are not what I need."

"I just can't offer you access."

"Get on the phone to Donaldson now," she ordered.

The man picked up the phone and dialed a number.

"Put him on speaker," Dani demanded.

Caplan complied, and the phone rang.

"Donaldson," a gruff voice answered.

"Mr. Donaldson, this is Danielle Traylor. Do you know who I am?"

A pause on the other end of the line. "Yes, ma'am, I do."

"Good."

"But you are not a member of the board, nor are you employed by Traylor Tech."

"That changed this week," Dani stated. "As of now, I'm the acting CEO."

"I don't understand."

"You won't have to if I don't get any cooperation."

"Jake, she says Vincent and Carlee Traylor died the other day," Caplan explained.

"I hadn't heard that," Donaldson replied incredulously.

"Imagine what that news would do to the stock prices?" Dani pointed out.

There was a pause. "I'm going to run this up the chain," Donaldson replied at last. His voice shook. No doubt there was some concern that either decision he made would be wrong.

"Fine," Dani answered. "But right now, we have a pressing problem."

"What?" Donaldson asked.

"There is an investigation into this facility, and as the new CEO, I need to get ahead of it."

"What are you talking about?" the operations officer asked over the speaker.

"An order for thirty small nuclear missiles."

"The Spikes?" Donaldson questioned.

"Yes," she acknowledged.

"What about them?"

"Mr. Donaldson, who authorized the manufacture of those missiles?" Dani asked.

"Uh," Donaldson mumbled. "I don't have the paperwork, but it would have come from the top."

"From what we are learning, the US government didn't order the weapons. Nor is there any record outside this plant to show they exist."

"That's not possible," Caplan exclaimed. "It would take an executive order to make that happen."

Dani turned to look at the security chief. "Exactly," she replied. "And the only person who can refute that one was made exploded on the Gulf of Mexico."

"That can't be," Donaldson iterated.

"Where are those Spikes?" Dani asked.

I forced back a smile as I watched the woman work. She possessed the very qualities that a company like this needed to run it. She'd have made a good Marine.

"Caplan, those are supposed to ship out," Donaldson remarked.

"When?" Dani asked.

"The order was ready. I'm not sure when."

Caplan grabbed the mouse to his computer and opened the screen. He typed in a password and leaned toward the monitor.

"It shows they are still here, Jake," Caplan offered.

Donaldson breathed a sigh of relief.

"Can we see them?" Dani requested. "They need to be put on hold until we figure out what happened."

There was a pause before Donaldson replied, "Under the highest scrutiny, Tom."

Caplan picked his head up and looked at me. "You'll need to turn over your firearm."

I gave the man a nod and pulled the forty-five off my belt.

"Ms. Traylor," Donaldson said. "I'm going to make that call now."

"I suggest you do," she sighed. We didn't know what or who Donaldson might call. If he had the right source, he could confirm the Traylor's boat went down. He might also find that Traylor intentionally left Dani out of any inheritance. We gambled that hadn't happened or, at least, that hadn't been confirmed yet.

"Until then, I'm following Mr. Caplan to put my eyes on these missiles." She nodded to Caplan to disconnect the call. The security chief realized he obeyed her without question a second after hanging up on his boss.

I handed my gun over to Caplan, who put the M45 in his drawer. "Follow me," he said, escorting us out of his office.

"How long have you worked here?" Dani asked.

"I've been with Traylor Tech for eight years, but I worked up in Baltimore. I came down here when they opened the plant last year."

"Have any problems here?" I asked.

He shook his head. "No, this has been a dream location. The local workforce is great. We brought in our own security team and engineers. The rest of the openings were filled here. Traylor Tech is paying out more than anyone else in the area, so we avoid having too many issues with turnover and theft. No one wants to lose a gig like this."

He led us through an open area with conveyor belts and assembly machinery. The equipment sat quietly down at the moment.

"How many—uh, products do you manufacture here?" I asked.

"I can't say."

Caplan didn't expound if he couldn't say because the details were classified or he didn't know.

"But you don't run twenty-four seven?"

"No, we run out orders. If we don't have an order, we work on maintenance and stocking."

"Stocking?" Dani asked.

"Components. Some parts are manufactured according to Traylor Tech specs. Those are all proprietary, and we manufacture them ourselves."

"Such as?" she asked.

He turned to study her. "I'd rather let Mr. Donaldson explain that to you. My job is securing the plant."

We entered another area. The lights were on here, and I counted eight men working. Most of what they were doing appeared to be cleanup and organization.

"Tom, what are you doing here?" one man asked. He was in his thirties, and judging from the clipboard he was reviewing, he might have been in charge of the team.

"We need to put a hold on that order of Spikes."

The man's face contorted. "A hold? Why?" he asked.

Caplan glanced at Dani, weighing what he could tell his coworker. "Mr. Donaldson and Ms. Traylor, here, want to verify a few things." He used Dani's name like a scapegoat, hoping the discussion would end.

"Tom, that order shipped out of here."

"When?" I asked.

"Half an hour. Maybe less."

Dani turned to look at me. "Mother fucker!" she blurted out. "We were already here."

20

"Where's it going?" I demanded.

The man with the clipboard stared at me blankly.

"Caplan, we need to know where it's going," Dani snapped.

"Jason, do you have the shipping paperwork?"

Our sudden animation drew the attention of a couple of the workers. A few exchanged odd glances, perhaps wondering what the excitement was we brought to a normally quiet night shift.

"Hang on," Jason replied. He flipped through the pages on the clipboard. "The driver just signed the shipping paperwork."

A forklift rumbled toward us. Wooden pallets stacked up on the forks rattled as the driver drove toward us.

"Here," Jason announced. "It's heading to Progreso."

If he was going to say anything else, it was drowned out by the sudden revving of the forklift and a squeal of tires. The vehicle turned sharply toward us. Its sudden change of direction sent most of the pallet tower teetering toward us.

Instinct sent me into Dani, shoving her back and diving after her. Wood crashed down where we were, and I heard a sickening crunch—the sound of flesh being crushed.

My head turned to see the forks pressing down on a fallen Jason.

"Move!" I shouted to Dani.

The forklift driver bounded off the seat with a long claw hammer used for sealing and opening wooden crates. The man, a Caucasian guy in his thirties, stalked toward Caplan who was under a couple of pallets. He pushed the top one off still confused by what just happened. The driver pulled his hand back as Caplan registered him. The former Ranger moved to his hip for the Beretta strapped in a holster. Before he could get his hands on the gun, the claw end of the hammer sliced through the air, impaling the security chief in the temple.

Dani let out a scream, and I grabbed her back, pushing her to run away. She sprinted forward, dodging around a stack of wooden crates. I got around the boxes as the gunshot echoed in the warehouse.

"What the hell?" someone shouted. Another gunshot, and I heard a body fall.

"We need to go!" I exclaimed.

Two more gunshots, neither directed at us. The driver was killing whoever wasn't helping him. Then he'd come after us. If I assumed he had Caplan's Beretta and it was fully loaded, then he started with about fifteen rounds. That left him about eleven. Since my forty-five was in Caplan's office he had me outgunned.

I pointed toward the double doors leading into the darkened manufacturing area. "We need to get there," I whispered. "Count to ten and run."

Before she could say anything, I stuck my head around the corner. The driver stood near the pile of pallets holding Caplan's gun. Across the aisle from me was a warehouse rack filled with what I assumed were outgoing shipments. It didn't offer the cover that the wooden crate did, but I wanted to draw his fire long enough to get Dani into the other area. I counted two other guys still standing and assumed they were all working together. If we were lucky, the security team wasn't in on this, and they'd be coming to the rescue soon.

If we were unlucky, they were all in on the scheme, and we had no cavalry coming for us.

The numbers in my head rolled from one to eight. I bolted across the opening as bullets whizzed through the air, peppering the pallets behind me. The driver continued firing his Beretta wildly. I dropped down in a slide behind the rack.

"She's getting away!" someone shouted

"Get her!" the driver shouted.

I was scrambling to my feet as one man launched into a pursuit of Dani. Since the only gun I'd seen so far was Caplan's, I hoped the man chasing Dani was still unarmed. It didn't make her safe, but at least it meant that he'd need to get right up on her to hurt her.

That wasn't true of the forklift driver. The only consolation I had was he didn't appear to be trained. Or, at least, he didn't spend a lot of time practicing. That didn't help me though. He still had at least eight or nine rounds to try to improve his aim. I didn't have anything.

I ran along the rack, keeping the metal shelving between the driver and myself. He'd stopped shooting while I was moving. He might realize he was limited on ammunition, and he needed to make the best of what he had. Of course, the man had the luxury of taking his time—a lesson he seemed to learn.

When I reached the end of the passage, I found myself facing a wall. Over my shoulder, I saw the driver stalking toward me. I scanned the area for anything I could use to protect myself. The best weapon I could improvise was a broken slat off a pallet. That wouldn't do much against a nine-millimeter.

However, my eyes lighted upon a large industrial electrical box. I'm not much of an electrician, but I recognized the high voltage symbol even if it was in Spanish. On the box was a large handle that read, *"Interruptor Eléctrico Principal."*

It was thirty feet from me and behind a rack of shelves probably installed to create a barrier. No one wants an errant forklift to crash into the building's main power supply. It could have disastrous effects.

I didn't have anything to crash into it. Instead, I broke into a sprint. I heard the gunshot behind me. My body didn't slow as I hit the metal box with a *thunk*. The impact jarred me, and I slipped. On the way down, I grabbed the giant switch, pulling it down with me. There was a clunk as the metal contacts inside the switch lost connection. Immediately, the lights in the warehouse went dark.

"Fuck!" a voice shouted in the dark.

I crawled to my feet moving away from the electrical switch. Hopefully, I'd leveled the playing field a little. Across the building, a simultaneous clicking sounded as emergency lights came on. Since I hadn't given any of this plan more than a millisecond of consideration, I hadn't thought about the battery-powered lights coming on.

That didn't matter. They only offered a fraction of the lighting the main overhead lights had. But they offered enough for the forklift driver and his remaining goon to find the switch and turn the lights back on.

As if on cue, the driver shouted, "Get the power back on!"

I was deep in the shadows, making me invisible. After lowering myself into a crouch, I crept toward the power supply. The other man moved in the same direction, but he wasn't attempting to remain quiet. The men might think I was defenseless since there were two of them. Add in the Beretta, and they might feel invincible.

Most people found confidence in having the upper hand. Illusions of power bolstered men when caution should prevail. Sure, the driver had a gun, and I didn't. But once the lights went out, the gun was virtually useless—especially given what I saw of his skill. Still, they considered me unarmed and therefore nothing more than prey. By cutting the power, it only proved to them I was in hiding.

As the second man approached, I leaped forward from the shadows. My forearm wrapped around the man's throat, and I pulled him back, buckling his knees. The

shock of impact scared the man, and I felt the panic rise
in him as he flailed his hands at me.

The driver must have seen my attack, and he fired at the
last place I'd been. But I'd dragged the other man back into
the dark, hiding us from the driver. We crashed into what
felt like a wooden crate, and the other man tried to get
his feet under him. With a solid stance, I jerked down on
the man as I tightened my grip around his throat. When
we both hit the concrete floor, I twisted his body to put
him mostly face down. Now that I had more leverage, I
wrenched my arm around until I felt the crack as his neck
broke.

The lifeless form slid out of my arm, and I was back on
my feet moving farther into the dark.

"Shit! Shit! Shit!" the driver mumbled. Another
mistake. I couldn't see him in the dark, but now I had the
sound of his voice to follow.

"We have your friend!" he shouted. I assumed he meant
Dani, and even if the man chasing her had gotten to
her before the lights were out, they hadn't returned. Not
unless they did so silently. If Dani was that quiet, then
there wasn't much I could do for her anyway.

So, I ignored him. Instead, I stayed low, avoiding any
lights. The technique produced fewer shadows. It took
me a couple of seconds to find the forklift driver, but
when I did see him, he was spinning wildly about with the
nine-millimeter extended. He couldn't see anything. That
was obvious from the rapid, sporadic swinging around.
While I couldn't see his face, I expected it was covered in
fear and disbelief. Now was the moment he realized the

gun in his hand didn't protect him. If I guessed, he wanted to run for it, but even that required him to venture into the unknown. This wasn't someone who knew what to do when he lost control.

Silently, I inched within ten feet of him. On all fours with my fingertips barely caressing the cold concrete floor, I prepared to attack. He twisted around 180 degrees from me. I covered the ten feet with two strides in less than a second.

The driver heard me coming a fraction of a second too late. He jerked around, keeping his right arm extended with the Beretta tightly gripped in his hand. I caught the man by the wrist, braced my feet, and yanked him toward me. The Beretta fired, but I held his arm straight, keeping the weapon aimed into the dark.

When he came forward, I used our countering momentums to slam my forehead into his face. He grunted with the blow, losing any footing he had. My left hand grabbed him on his left side just above his kidney. In a second, I rotated my entire body lifting him into a modified judo throw. The driver slammed into the concrete, and I heard the Beretta hit the floor half a second later. He sucked in a gasp of air, and I released him, scampering after the gun.

My fingers traced along the concrete until I brushed up against it. As I raised up, my finger slipped into the trigger guard. Turning, I leveled the gun at the man's silhouette as he tried to push himself to his feet. Without a thought, I squeezed the trigger. The muzzle flash illuminated the driver's distorted face. When the darkness overtook me again, it seemed blacker than a few seconds earlier.

I debated restoring the power but considered the advantage it gave me over the last man searching for Dani. There was enough light from the emergency lighting to find the exit.

The next room was the dormant manufacturing space. Shapes loomed in the eerie lighting from the machinery, and I followed the faint glow emanating from a window across the plant.

When I reached the light, I found a door leading back into the offices. The lighting in here was limited to only the far end of the hallway. Someone was moving across the corridor, blocking the light for a second.

"Find her?" I asked in a low voice.

It didn't even come close to matching the forklift driver's voice. The guy at the other end must not have been paying attention. He responded, "Not yet. What happened to the lights?"

He stood in the middle of the hallway staring into the darkness at me. I raised the Beretta, and he obviously couldn't see me. The muzzle flashed again, and the man fell backward.

"Dani!" I shouted. "It's clear."

A few seconds passed, and I heard her respond. "Chase?"

The voice came from past the dead man in the hall, and I jogged past him to find a more illuminated corridor with three doors. The last one opened, and Dani stuck her head out. She saw me alone and ran to my arms.

The lights came back on, and the door behind me burst open. Two security guards appeared aiming their own Berettas at us.

21

The Beretta dropped to the floor, and I kept my hands around Dani.

"Don't move!" one guard shouted. "What the hell is going on?"

I glanced over at him to see the guard from the entrance and another man standing in the hallway.

"You need to call for help," I told them. "These men shot Caplan and the other men."

"You have the gun," the one from the gate pointed out.

"I told you who I was," Dani said, pushing away from me. "These men tried to kill us."

"Tom was a Ranger," the guy pointed out.

"It was an ambush," I explained. "None of us saw it coming."

"But you survived."

"Only because they went after Caplan first," I explained. It was true, too. If the forklift driver had come after me first, he might have had enough of an advantage. Although, I suspected that even with Caplan, the only advantage he had was that he pinned the chief of security under the pallets before Caplan could react.

Despite the outcome, the forklift driver had been smart about his attack. He knew Caplan was armed, and he might have known enough to deduce that he was the only one with a gun. Kill him first and take his weapon. It would just be a matter of mopping up the rest of us.

I was glad I didn't make it that easy, though.

"What's your name?" Dani demanded, trying to find the forceful demeanor she'd displayed earlier. It didn't seem to matter now. There were several dead men between here and the loading dock. This stepped beyond being worried about his job. This was a clusterfuck.

"Ms. Traylor, I'm going to need you to move over here."

"Do what he says," I urged her.

"What the hell do we do?" the other guard asked.

"When Tank and Collins get back, we put these two in the secured rooms until I can call for support."

"But Tom's dead," the other guard pointed out.

"I'm aware. Now shut the fuck up."

Two more men showed up at the other end of the hallway. Both carried the same ex-military look that these did. Tank and Collins.

"It's a fucking mess!" one said. "Tom and Jason are dead. The whole shift."

"Let's get them put someplace," the head guard from the front gate announced.

"Listen, there's a shipment of missiles that just left here," Dani stated. "You guys gave them to terrorists."

The man studied her. "Ma'am, I'm not sure what you want me to do." I heard a hint of a Southern accent in his voice. He'd lost a lot of the twang over the years, but it still lingered.

"Let me call my contact at the CIA," I begged. "He can stop the truck."

He shook his head. "Until I figure out what the hell is going on, you aren't making a call yet. Not until I figure out what the hell is going on."

"It will be too late," Dani pleaded.

"Ms. Traylor, the sooner you let me get to work, the sooner I can do what I need to do."

He was just a soldier, or, at least, he had been. Never a leader, and right now, he needed orders to tell him what to do. I didn't fault him for that. The US military trained hundreds of thousands of non-coms only to follow orders. This poor guy was too young to have made a career out of the military, and nothing he'd done identified what branch he served under. The kid did a few tours and used it to get a decent security gig only a few hours from the beach. He never intended to be the one to solve the problems.

"Dani, do what he says," I told her after several seconds.

The guard regarded me with a hint of gratitude. That vanished as he stepped into action. I had to give him credit for staying on task. He seemed to realize that he had an absolute disaster under his roof.

"Come on," one of the other guards ordered me away from Dani. He motioned for me to grab the wall, and when I complied, he frisked me. The man removed the cellphone that Smith gave me.

"Wait, this is an emergency," Dani blurted out again.

"What the hell do you think we have here?" the main guard snapped.

He motioned for them to take me, and they marched me away from Dani. I suspected she would be out of harm's way for the time being. So far, they didn't understand how or if she fit into the organization, but she still had the Traylor name. No one wanted to rub the boss the wrong way.

However, for every minute they detained us, the missiles got farther from us. While I had no intention at first of becoming the CIA's lackey, allowing thirty small nukes loose scared me. I'd carried Spike missiles in the past. Those were merely anti-aircraft ones designed to take out a chopper or disable a tank. They fit into a pack, and I toted one around the hills of Afghanistan for six weeks with minimal effort.

These Traylor Tech Spikes were just as small. Only they carried a core that could take out a city block. Not to mention whatever radioactive residue it would leave. Anyone could hide one in a suitcase and drive it across the border. In two days, someone could stand on Pennsylvania Avenue and launch a nuke into the White House. With thirty of them, they could put them all over the world.

The one called Tank directed me into an office. They didn't cuff me, which might mean they didn't see me as a threat or a simple mistake. Only a desk and a chair occupied the room, and it was obvious that no one was using it. It made me wonder how many administrative staff this plant had. Extra offices allowed them to grow staff later if the need arose.

Tank shut the door, and since no one designed the office to function as a prison, he stood sentry in the hallway. Another mistake. Without eyes on me, I could do anything. Which I did. I searched the drawers, only to find the desk was as empty as the office. Not even a stray paper clip. In fact, I thought the furniture might have been fresh out of the box.

As I sank into the office chair, I considered what the options we had were. Smith should be in Merida by now or, at least, soon. He'd be reaching out, but without the phone, I wouldn't be able to answer.

The guy—they called him Jason—said the missiles were being shipped to Progreso. That only made sense if they were moving them on a ship. If they were going to drive them out of Mexico, the quickest route would be toward Guatemala or Belize. Even that left them on the road for long enough to be intercepted. A ship would be faster, as long as no one was looking for it. I assumed the forklift driver and his small crew were supposed to eliminate any trace of the shipment. That wouldn't be an arduous task. Destroy any record. They wouldn't have to kill everyone either. At best, just Jason, since he probably filled out the paperwork. They might have intended to kill him off-site. Unfortunately for everyone, Dani and I showed up too soon, forcing them to improvise.

The door opened, and the head guard, who seemed to have taken charge stepped inside. Tank still stood in the corridor.

"I just watched the surveillance video."

"Are you satisfied we didn't start it?" I asked.

"Yeah, I could see it was not you," he admitted. "I still don't know what to do with it."

I stared at him as I leaned back in the desk chair. "You served?" I asked.

He nodded. "Army," he replied, adding, "Infantry."

"Marine Recon," I told him. "This is bigger than what happened here."

"That's what Ms. Traylor keeps saying, but I searched for her on the internet. She's Vincent Traylor's daughter, but according to Google, it says they were estranged."

"Yeah, she is and was, but right now, she's also the only remaining Traylor left alive. That will likely mean she's the head of this company. Or she will be very soon."

"She said the people who have the missiles killed her father."

I nodded. "What's your name?" I asked.

"Chris Jordan."

"Chris, these people now have access to thirty handheld nuclear missiles. Any of which can be carried in a backpack. Do you know what kind of damage that can cause?"

"Yeah, I do."

I continued, "Listen, I have a CIA contact. If we can reach out to him, we might stop them before they ship them out."

"No offense, Mr.—uh, what was your name?"

"Gordon."

"Mr. Gordon," Chris explained, "I'm at a loss as to who to trust at this point. You didn't start killing anyone, but everything is suspicious. I've got a call into the corporate security. Without Caplan, I'm trying to figure out what to do."

"You didn't call the local police?" I asked.

He shook his head. "Not yet. But I have to do something soon."

I agreed with him. If he didn't bring in the local law enforcement soon, it would draw more suspicion. Somehow, he also realized what kind of scrutiny that would bring down on the company. There was more to this soldier than just grunt work. Unfortunately, I wondered if he wasn't searching for how he could land on top with the company.

"Where is that truck going?" I asked.

"The paperwork shows it going to Progreso."

I knew that already. "It doesn't say anything more?"

His face scrunched up in disgust. "The shipping form was—uh—covered in blood."

"There's only one port there," I pointed out.

Chris nodded.

"I need to stop them," I urged. "You know that."

"This is too fucked up for me to let you go," he remarked, waving his arm back as if the carnage in the warehouse was right there.

"Let me call my contact. He can get things moving."

Chris let his head droop. He was in a tight spot. I didn't know him, but my instinct got a sense of him. The former infantryman found himself in a precarious position. There was going to be hell to pay from somewhere for the dead bodies in the plant. It wouldn't shock me if the company wanted to cover it up, leaving him in an even more tangled quandary. At the same time, he realized the threat of sending thirty missiles off with terrorists.

"I don't understand how they did this," he murmured.

"Right now, it looks like it was an inside job. Vincent Traylor, himself, arranged the order. His authority could get around any questions or security concerns. Either he tried to raise the price or balked on the deal. Whichever happened, it wasn't an acceptable choice for his buyers."

"Shit," Chris whispered. "That's bad."

"Yeah, and if we don't get a handle on it, this will blow up in the press. Pardon my pun."

He fished the prepaid cellphone from his pocket. "I have to call the local authorities," he admitted.

I nodded. "There are a lot of cameras here," I noted.

"Yeah."

"I'm sorry then. You're doing the best you can." I let my shoulders slump as I said that.

"Sorry for what?"

Then I head-butted him. I did not intend to do a lot of damage, so instead of slamming my forehead into something that would give way, like his nose, I cracked our foreheads together. The result rang both of our bells. Only I was prepared for the disorientation, and I stepped back and swung my fist into his temple.

The guard crashed into the desk and slid toward the floor. I swooped down and pulled his Beretta from the holster on his hip, turning as soon as the barrel was clear. Tank burst through the door to stare down the muzzle.

"On your knees!" I ordered.

Tank glowered at me for a second before shifting his eyes to Chris, who lay sprawled on the floor. He lowered himself to his knees.

"Hands on your head!"

The man complied, and I moved around him. He was named Tank for a reason, and it wasn't his diminutive stature. Because of that, I didn't want to give him enough space to grab or swing at me. His barrel-sized arms might knock me out with a swipe.

Once I was behind him, I reached to his belt where he kept a pair of cuffs.

"I'd suggest next time you cuff your prisoners," I advised him as I slapped the bracelets on both of his wrists. I pulled his Beretta from the holster along with the extra magazine he had on his belt. With the gun still trained on him, I moved around and picked up the cellphone Chris dropped when I hit him.

"Tell him I'm sorry I had to do that. It was for his own good."

Tank only growled. I gave him a smile before I sprinted out the door.

22

I was in the Mustang, racing toward the gate before I pulled out the cellphone. The guards had abandoned the gate after they converged on us in the warehouse, and I didn't slow for the wooden arm. The hood slipped under the arm, allowing the wood to slam against the windshield. Surprisingly, the glass didn't crack on impact, and the car snapped the arm off.

As I sped away from the plant, the headlights splayed out into the dark. I fumbled for the cellphone and dialed Smith's number.

"Where are you?" I demanded as soon as he answered the phone.

"I'm on the ground in Merida," he responded. "Did you get to the factory?"

"That's a disaster," I stated. "The missiles are on a truck heading toward Progreso."

"Shit, Gordon. What happened?"

"They left minutes before we got there," I explained, annoyed that he even asked.

"Where in Progreso?"

"Don't know," I responded as I shifted into fifth gear and revved the gas. "I'd guess the port. Make a phone call and find out what ships plan to sail by morning."

"What makes you think it's a ship?"

I rolled my eyes, a futile gesture since the CIA man was on the phone. "It's the only way to get them out. If they were flying them out, they'd go to the airport in Merida. That would draw more scrutiny."

"Fine, I'll see what I can find out."

Before he could ask me anything else, I disconnected to focus on the drive. Luckily, Mexico provided adequate signage, and I could follow the arrows pointing me toward Progreso. The late hour offered empty roads, and I pressed the accelerator to the floor.

It took me an hour and a half to reach the city, and I slowed as I passed the city limits.

"What have you found out?" I asked when Smith answered the phone.

"There's only one ship leaving port. It's shipping henequen fibers to Gulfport, Mississippi."

"Henequen fibers?" I questioned.

The CIA agent chuckled. "I thought you'd ask that. It's the product of a plant in Mexico. They use the fibers for all sorts of goods. Hats, clothes, packing material. That kind of thing."

"That's the only ship?" I asked.

"Yeah."

"Shit, that has to be it," I remarked.

"Well, we can't prove it," Smith pointed out. "I can have it searched when it reaches the States."

"Hell, they can offload it in the middle of the Gulf," I suggested. "We're talking about three or four crates."

"Doesn't mean they will, though."

"Or we can get on board and put our eyes on them."

"We don't have that kind of authority," Smith advised.

"I don't need it," I reminded him.

"Port security might be tough. There's only one way in, and it's a two-mile levee."

"Which means they won't be watching the water," I suggested. "I need some equipment."

"It's one in the morning," Smith retorted. "I don't have anything just lying around. What do you need?"

"Full scuba set—BCD, regulator, air. And a scooter."

"Scooter?" Smith questioned.

"Yeah, it's a two-mile swim otherwise."

"Where do you expect me to find that?"

"We just need a dive shop. We can steal it," I told him. "I'd expect the CIA to compensate the shop tomorrow, though."

Smith groaned.

"Look, you could have left me alone on Isla Mujeres, Smith. But no, you wanted some help to clean up your mess."

"Fine, let me find something."

He went silent for a minute while I assumed he was searching for a shop.

"Here's one on Calle 39," he told me. "Meet me there in ten minutes."

It only took me seven to find a spot down the street. I walked up to the back door of the shop. There was a

camera focused on the alley behind Yucatán Divers, but
it pointed toward the door. I was betting that it was only
recording on site. Progreso wasn't a large city, and any
twenty-four-hour security monitoring would be a small
company. At least, I hoped that was the case.

No matter what the surveillance was, I needed to be in
and out of the store in less than five minutes. I'd already
thought it out. The shop would have a rental section
where the employees kept all the regularly maintained
equipment. I knew what I needed, but I wanted to wait
for Smith.

After all, if I made sure he was involved, the man
would go a little farther to ensure the shop didn't react by
calling law enforcement down on me. Plus, it was a lot of
equipment, and I needed a couple of extra hands to bring
it out.

The agent arrived three minutes later.

"So we just go in?" he asked.

The door was a solid wood door, but the frame was
old. It was the classic feint—a strong door added to a
crumbling facade. Perceived security.

I stepped back before driving the sole of my shoe into the
door. I landed the kick to the side of the doorknob. The
impact splintered the wooden door jamb, and I thought
I'd make sure that when Smith had it replaced, he added a
steel frame to prevent this sort of break-in.

"Come on," I urged as we stepped inside.

There was no alarm that started blaring, but that didn't
mean we hadn't triggered a silent one. Time was now

of the utmost essence, and I hurried through the dark hallways.

I'd been in hundreds of dive shops across the Caribbean, and almost all of them kept their rental gear in the back. The stores often made more money on the used equipment than the sales of new gear, and they'd rent it out over and over, wearing the stuff down. It wasn't something they wanted people to see when they wanted to buy a $1500 buoyancy control device.

Yucatan Divers was no different. As soon as we were in the door, we found ourselves in a back room with the air-filling station—an intricate network of larger cylinders and an electric pump designed to fill the scuba tanks with filtered air. It took just a second to figure out which tanks were filled and which were empty, waiting on refills. Someone printed the words "*lleno*" and "*vacio*" on the walls over two groupings of cylinders. Despite my meager Spanish, I guessed that "*vacio*" might mean vacant or empty.

"Grab two of those," I ordered Smith, pointing to the ones under the word, "*lleno.*" It reminded me of *chiles rellenos*, and I chuckled. Filled chile peppers. Most bilingual people would compare me to an idiot, but that realization made me feel almost brilliant.

Smith obeyed me, picking up two cylinders by the valves and carrying them outside. After I riffled through the rows of BCDs hanging on a steel pipe, I found an extra-large. I snatched it off the hanger, grabbed a regulator hanging on a wire rack. My arm slid into the BCD, and I draped the hoses around my neck. The only things I still needed were some extra weights, fins, and a scooter.

The weights were hanging on a belt on the wall next to a bin of fins. I pulled a belt filled with lead off the nail the shop improvised as a hook before picking out two matching shoe fins. There was a closet with "*motos*" painted in block letters on the door. When I opened it, I found several small electric scooters hanging on a wooden shelf. I pulled one off, a Waydoo Subnado. The device could move about two miles per hour according to the label on the casing.

I rested the scooter across my shoulder and ran out of the store. Smith was at the end of the street with the trunk to a nearly identical Volkswagen.

"Did you rent the same car?" I asked as I loaded the gear into his back.

"No, I took the ferry over and drove. I only know one pilot, and he was too busy taking you and Ms. Traylor over."

I nodded.

"Where is she?" he asked, curiously.

"Still at the plant," I admitted. "We got separated, and I didn't have time to go back for her."

Smith gave me a curious look.

"The guards know who she is," I explained. "I don't think she's in any danger. But you might have to use your influence to get her free if they send her to the local jail."

He shrugged. "Where to?"

"We need to go to the beach. I'll have to wade out from there."

Smith nodded.

"Shit!" I exclaimed. "I forgot a mask."

I didn't wait for him, turning to sprint to the shop. In the distance, I heard a siren approaching, and I suspected we triggered some sort of alarm. As I ran into the store, I hurried to the front and grabbed a new Mares mask. As I turned to run back out, I paused in front of a display of flashlights. I picked up one attached to a wrist holder before I ran through the store and out the back entrance.

When I reached the Mustang, I saw the flashing of blue lights turning down the street. Without hitting the lights on the car, I drove around the corner, careful not to touch my brakes. Once out of sight of the arriving cops, I sped off and flipped the headlights on.

23

The surf lapped up over my feet as I shuffled out through the sand. Smith stood on the beach, preparing to go back to the car and wait. We didn't have any radios, and I hadn't even thought about needing one until we reached the beach. We decided that the only option was to go radio silent until I got off the ship. If the need arose, I could find the communications room on board the freighter.

The Gulf waters were warm—a good thing, since I didn't bother stealing a wetsuit while I was gearing up. It was shallow off the coast of Progreso, which meant I wouldn't get much deeper than twenty feet. Those depths stayed that way for miles out, which is what precipitated the need to build the two-mile port road. Now the village could be a destination for cruise ships and freighters when in the past, the only thing that sustained the population was fishing from small shallow-drafted vessels.

There was no moon out, and staring off across the sea, I knew it would be a dark run to the lights of the ship. When the surf was up to my chest, I stuck the second-stage regulator into my mouth and lowered my body into the sea. The Waydoo scooter splashed off my shoulder into the water, and I grabbed the handles. I reached over and ignited the flashlight on my wrist, giving me a narrow beam of light that spread out about ten feet in front of me.

Thankfully, the shallow waters would keep me out of a decompression dive, and I'd likely need to surface at least once to get my bearings, since, along with a wetsuit, I'd forgotten to get a compass.

The scooter hummed in my grip, and I increased the speed. My light stretched out along the sand. Several fish darted into the dark as I motored along. There was an eerie feeling of being inside that cone of light in the sea. I love night dives, but it can give off claustrophobic feelings. Progreso only had a few artificial reefs close to shore, and while that meant most of the big toothy fish shouldn't be close, it wasn't a guarantee.

Seconds clicked by in my head, turning into minutes. After ten minutes, I checked my depth. I was still at only fifteen feet. After adjusting the angle of the scooter, I allowed it to carry me to the surface, where for a split second I broke into the air long enough to get my bearings. As I submerged, I adjusted my heading to the east and sped up.

The battery gauge on the scooter was nothing more than a bar of six green lights. One had already gone dark, and the fifth one was flashing. It occurred to me that once I left the ship, I might have to make a long swim back if the battery died on the scooter. Most only lasted between one and two hours. I estimated it would take close to an hour to reach the ship. With any luck, there'd be enough battery to get me close to shore.

I surfaced twice more. Each time, I turned back to
the east. Despite my attempts to hold a straight heading,
the dark surroundings obscured any waypoints. Add in a
current, and I drifted off course.

Fifty-six minutes after entering the water, I slowed the
scooter and extinguished the light. On the surface, I moved
closer to the ship. The name, *Álmodozó*, reflected in white
lettering on the side. I didn't know what the word meant
or even the language.

I inched forward through the waves until I reached the
hull. In the pocket of my BCD, I removed a spool of line.
After inflating the BCD enough to keep it just below the
surface, I attached the scooter to it. With the other end, I
tied a quick knot to a recessed cleat in the metal hull. Using
the front clip on the BCD, I attached my fins and mask
to the inflatable vest. Now, everything would be right here
when I came back for it.

My head craned toward the sky to study the side
of the ship. The only way up was to scale the hull.
About midship, I noted some rungs leading up from
the waterline. They didn't reach the top deck, instead
stopping at a hatch halfway up.

I scaled up the ladder until I reached the hatch. It had
a lever on the outside for opening, and I pulled down on
it. The metal groaned as I stretched away from the rungs
to heave down. No one had oiled the latch in a long time,
and based on how firmly it held, the crew didn't open this
hatch much. After a bit of struggling, I felt the handle
give a little, and I redoubled my efforts to move the bar.
It rotated with a squeal until it was pointing toward the

sea below me. With a sigh of relief, I pulled the door open, revealing a dark aperture.

Once I climbed inside, I closed the hatch. The dive light remained strapped to my wrist, and when I turned it on, I found myself in a narrow opening. On my hands and knees, I crawled along the tunnel for about fifty feet until I came to a drop to the deck below. Before descending, I stuck my head down to ensure the corridor was empty. I slipped through the gap and fell down to land on my feet.

I was on a walkway overlooking several steel containers stacked in the hold. A retractable deck covered the area, allowing more containers to be stacked in the open air. A quick count told me there were fifteen containers down here, and no telling how many on the top deck. Each box was forty feet long. Since the crates I was looking for could fit into any of these, it would be like hunting for a needle in a haystack. Or, in this case, it was boxes of dried fibers.

There should be a manifest somewhere, and if I could get my hands on that, it would make searching the ship an easier task.

The only problem with finding the manifest was they were kept in the bridge. While we were still at the dock, it was unlikely the bridge was ever empty. Even more unlikely that I could walk in and ask for it like I was.

I found a metal staircase descending into the hold. No one appeared to be around. I guessed they were all up on deck.

If I continued aft, I should be able to find the engine room. I expected to find some crew there, and while I wanted to stay out of sight for as long as possible,

eventually I'd need to encounter someone. I preferred to
do that on my terms.

As I continued aft, I saw a door labeled. "*Gépház*."
While I had no clue what it meant, the symbol on the door
reminded me of a wrench. I opened the door and climbed
down the narrow metal stairs to the sound of mechanical
rumblings. The temperature rose as I got nearer to the
engines.

I paused on the steps to peek below. Two men were
performing some maintenance on the equipment. It
appeared they were taking readings on the motors. I slid
down the stairs without making a sound, an effort that
seemed pointless given how loud the room was. As I
moved around the engines, I kept the two crewmen on the
other side, using the large diesel motors to shield me from
their view.

A smile crept across my face when I saw what I was
looking for—a locker. Inside, I found an extra pair of
coveralls. I stepped into them, zipping up the front. There
was no nametag embroidered on the label, and I stretched
to pull the fabric tight. The uniform was one size too small
for me, but it would work. With any luck, no one would
notice the gap at my ankles where the pants didn't extend
all the way down. If they noticed that, they might see the
scuba boots on my feet too. At that point, the ruse would
be up.

Since I now felt disguised, I strolled around the engine
room. One crewman running diagnostics glanced up at
me. I gave him a silent nod. He returned the gesture before
going back to his work. A crew like this often had recent

additions. As long as I appeared to belong, I hoped I could get around.

I took the stairs back up, trying not to wear out my good fortune. It was three flights later that I stepped out onto the deck. A crane lowered another container onto the deck as three men prepared to lash the boxes to the ship with thick straps. I turned and found the stair leading up to the bridge and conning tower.

The door leading to the bridge opened in, and I climbed the steps to the tower. It occurred to me halfway up that whoever was on the bridge might speak Spanish or anything but English. This suddenly felt like a bad idea.

But I'd committed to it now. I stepped onto the bridge, and the lights of the displays and radars glowed in the dark room. After a second, I realized there were three people in the room, but they kept the lights out. It was a fact I should have realized. I'd been on carriers before but never on the bridge, and as I thought about it, I was certain I'd never been there at night. But if the lights on the bridge had been on, it would make it impossible to see out.

A stern-looking man several years older than me turned to stare at me when I entered. I gave it my best shot.

"*El jefe* sent me for the manifest," I stated, mixing my languages and lowering my voice to disguise any accent I might have.

The man that I figured for either the captain or the first officer pointed toward a binder on the table.

"*Gracias*," I replied, grabbing the folder and hurrying back out like a man on a mission.

My heart thudded in my chest as I hurried back down the stairs. I didn't want to give anyone time to remember not seeing me before. Or wonder who I was.

When I hit the deck, I crossed it in a rush, trying to get to the other side and remain out of sight of the bridge.

That shouldn't have worked.

I'm not one to look a gift horse in the mouth, and I stopped between the containers, opening the book.

At least it wasn't in Spanish, I considered as I stared at the page. It was, however, in another language. Something Slavic. Not something I could speak or read. At least with Spanish, I might make out twenty percent when I was reading.

I studied it in vain for several minutes, trying to decipher what everything meant. There were numbers, and after a bit, I guessed some referred to the container and then the next line registered the count of bails or boxes of fibers. With that in mind, I flipped through, looking for either the number three or thirty. If they listed only the crates, then there would be three.

Most things seemed to be classified as "*szál.*" There were pages and pages with that description. I paused when I read "*láda*" in a single column. My finger ran along the words to find the number three printed. I let out a sigh of relief.

Once I figured out I was looking for container seventy-two, I tucked the manifest under my arm and started searching for the box in question.

24

I was running out of time. There was no real rhyme or reason to how they numbered the containers, and the manifest did me no good. If it described where box seventy-two was, I didn't understand it.

After fifteen minutes, I'd walked up and down the rows on the top deck. So far, no seventy-two.

It must be in the lower holds. I'd passed three different crewmen as I made my search. Each time I pulled the manifest out and examined it as I checked the numbers. That seemed to placate any curiosities, but sooner or later, I'd run across someone who could call me out on my bullshit.

Once I got below deck, I let out a sigh. Container number seventy-two sat right in front of me. It was, unfortunately, stacked on top of number twenty-two. I looked around to find I was alone at the moment, and I found a rolling ladder that the crew used to strap down the steel boxes. After moving it over, I climbed up and found the container sealed with a wire clasp. It was easy to break. The doors swung open, and I crawled up into the container.

My flashlight lit up the inside, which was empty except for three boxes. It took a couple of minutes to pop the top off the crates. The first one contained molded foam designed to hold something shaped like an eighteen-inch missile.

But there were no missiles inside the crate. Only ten empty slots for them.

I moved to the next box. There I found five missiles and five empty slots. The third box was also empty.

What the hell?

Where were the Spikes? They only shipped five? Why bother shipping the empty containers?

It gave me a sick feeling in my stomach. What was the point? Why ship only five?

Something seemed to pop up in my head. It was a feint. They knew someone was closing in on them, so they sent the crates on to the ship. Expecting the CIA to chase the ship and search it. By the time the US government intercepted the vessel, the rest of the missiles would head off somewhere else.

Everything shifted. The rumbling of the engines grew louder as the propellers pushed the ship off the dock.

Shit. Time's up.

I needed to get off the boat now. But I turned back to look at the missiles still in the crate. There were only five. I didn't understand why they'd leave five. Unless they were shortchanging someone down the line. It seemed like a stupid move.

Right then, I decided to take the five with me. Even if all I did was drop them into the ocean, then Smith could

RED LIGHT AT NIGHT

send a team to retrieve them. But they needed to be off this ship.

The Spikes were small enough to be carried in a backpack, but I didn't have one. And five, even if considered handheld, were too many for me to tote out by hand. I needed to find something small enough for me to put them in.

The lockers in the engine room might hold something that would work. I moved to the door to step off onto the ladder. My foot froze over the edge as I realized the ladder was no longer where I left it.

Three men stared up at me from the floor below. Even in the dark of the cargo hold, I saw the pistol in one of their hands. He raised it and fired a second after I ducked back into the steel box. A ting of metal echoed in the metal chamber as the bullet ricocheted off the steel.

They were watching the box, just like they'd done at the plant. The people going after the missiles were leaving nothing to chance. They intended to wipe out any evidence that the missiles ever existed, let alone that they had them.

That thought stopped me in my tracks, and I turned to look back at the boxes. Five Spikes could level five square blocks of a city. Or they could easily obliterate a freighter. Hell, they'd already mastered that move with *Serendipity's Odyssey*. The ship blows up, and the evidence would sink to the bottom of the ocean.

There'd be no way to hide the nuclear detonation. Unless there was a way to blow the missiles without setting off the nuclear portion. Maybe they stripped the core out

of it. Or they just might not care. Even if there was a small
nuclear explosion, the military would register it, but by
the time they sent in the response team, the remnants of
the vessel and any evidence would be thousands of feet
underwater. Even if they undertook a salvage operation,
the answers to what happened would be months away. By
then, the other twenty-five missiles could be spread across
the globe. Or parked all within the DC Beltway.

Another gunshot sent a round pinging off the ceiling
of container seventy-two. I backed up into the container.
Unarmed, they pinned me down. They must have
assumed at first I had a gun, and by now they might know,
at least minimally, that the crew they left at the plant was
dead. That would lead them to be a little cautious in their
approach, but in a few minutes when I hadn't returned
fire, they'd suspect correctly that I was a sitting duck.

Unless I wanted to fire a nuke at them, but that seemed
counterproductive inside the hold of a ship. I needed
another way out, and whatever method I intended to
take needed to happen now. I edged along the wall of
the box. When I peered out, I spotted two men below.
Each had retreated toward the opposite edges of the stack
of containers across from me. One raised his weapon
and fired again, but I pulled back before he squeezed the
trigger.

The two men shouted to each other, but the voices
echoed through the din of the diesel engines churning us
away from Progreso.

There was about a ten-foot span across the aisle to the
next row of containers. Even if I was another ten to fifteen

feet higher, there was little chance of me making a jump like that. A vision of me falling face-first into the deck played out in my mind.

The inside of the container was smooth metal, a contrast to the outside that had girders and beams tying between the edges. If I got around to the side, I could climb up or down the box. There was no chance the two gunmen below would give me the seconds I needed to get to the side. Even if I got out, they'd have a clear line of sight on me.

I grabbed the closest wooden crate, which carried the five Spike missiles in it. After pulling it around straight, I grabbed the backside and shoved it toward the opening.

My voice shouted, "This fucker's armed."

The cry echoed off the metal boxes a second before the wooden crate toppled out of the opening, dropping twelve feet to the floor with a crash. I didn't wait or even take a look. Instead, I leaped from the opening, grabbing the top of the left door. My impact swung it around on the hinge and used the momentum to throw my body around to the outside. The gunshots below sounded a second later, and the metal rang out like a gong with each bullet. When the door hit the apex of its swing, I let go and grabbed the outside edge. My right foot missed the girder, and I caught my weight with my hands, pulling myself back up.

There was no time to catch my breath, and with the door still swaying back and forth, I used it to shield myself as I scaled to the top of the container. My arms pulled me up, and I rolled onto the roof as one shooter, realizing what I was doing, moved to get a better aim.

On my back, I turned to stare down the line of four containers to the end. I needed to make it to the end. The opening I'd come through earlier was on the catwalk overlooking the cargo hold. It would be impossible to get up on the walkway and into the opening without offering a perfect target.

No, I needed to get to the steps and make it topside. Even now, we were getting farther from shore, and every minute I waited made it that much farther of a swim.

I rolled to my feet and sprinted across the top of the container, leaping over the three-to-four-foot gap between the rows. Metal clunked as my feet slammed onto the next one, and I continued forward. The two men below shouted back and forth, and from the way their voices followed, they were pursuing me from below.

When I reached the next to last container, I turned, angling my run aft toward the metal staircase leading up to the top deck. As I reached the closest corner to the stairs, I launched myself off the top of the container. The handrail was only about seven feet away—a long jump for me. I hoped that while the distance was far, the angle toward the staircase made it attainable.

Instead, I slammed into the bar at an awkward direction. My hands tried to grab the metal, but the round steel banister slipped through my grasp. I fell backward, flailing for a split second, out of control.

When I crashed down, I landed on something not quite soft that grunted. The man I hadn't seen lay crumpled underneath me. I rolled off him as one gunman came into view. He appeared only a few feet from me, and lowering my shoulder, I launched into him, driving him into the container behind him.

As he slumped down, I pivoted on my left foot and ran aft toward the door to the engine room. The door leading to the lower decks slammed open when I shoved my hand against it. I didn't enter, though. Instead, I ran past it, sliding between two containers as footsteps ran up the aisle. When I heard the door open and shut again, I took off for the stairs.

The two men I'd put on the ground were still there, but the gunman regained his senses and climbed to his feet as I ascended the stairwell. Two gunshots exploded behind me as I crested the landing and shoved through the door into the night air.

It took a split second for me to get my bearings, but I ran forward, crossing the deck to the opposite side. With the wind and engine noises bouncing off the water, I couldn't hear the door I'd just busted through open, but I assumed the guy with the gun made it up the steps behind me.

There was no way to return to take the Spikes without taking out both gunmen, and now I felt the effects of the fall I'd taken.

The freighter was moving now at several knots, and Progreso, already two miles from the dock, was receding into the darkness. There was no way the scooter would have enough juice to get me back, even if I got to it as the ship picked up speed.

But I couldn't stay on the ship, and as I hit the rail, I jumped, letting my feet touch the top rail as I went over.

Another gunshot sounded behind me as I vanished into
the blackness below.

25

The dark water swallowed me, and I kicked down. I hit the water near the forward port side. When I surfaced, the hull bore down on me, and I stroked away in desperation. The surge of the freighter dragged me back, and if I didn't stay away, it could pull me under the hull.

The current sucked at me, and I thrashed harder, trying to stay off the hull. As the ship moved past, the drag grew stronger as the propellers pushed the sea behind it.

Something scraped across my face, and I realized it was the line I'd attached to the hull earlier. The rope fed back under the ship as the BCD and my gear dangled toward the rotating prop. I struggled to get away, but it was a losing battle. With the line in my hand, I let the surge pull me under. It wasn't so much letting as just failing to stop it.

As I slid down the rope, I felt the BCD. My hand searched in the blackness for the regulator, and once I found it, I shoved it into my mouth, sucking in a breath of filtered, condensed air.

The BCD bounced off the hull, and if I held on to it, I wouldn't get pulled through the propeller wash as the back

of the boat. But that wasn't sustainable either. I'd run out
of air.

I had to get away from the boat. First thing I needed to
do was get the BCD on my torso. The scooter detached,
and I didn't bother trying to hold on to it. The tube
tumbled out of my grip into the abyss.

When I unhooked the strap at the front, I felt the mask
slip off into the deep before I could catch it. I snagged one
fin before it sank, but lost the other. As I gripped the BCD,
I worked my arms into the vest until I fastened myself into
it.

The sea water plowed past me, dragging me up against
the hull. I struggled to put the one fin on my right foot,
thinking that I would want to swim toward the port side
and that put the fin on the opposite side to push me. Some
part of me worried for a split second that I'd only go in
a circle for a few seconds before being pulverized by the
prop.

I turned on the flashlight, still attached to my wrist.
By rotating around and pulling the line around my waist,
I saw the moving water about sixty feet aft, where two
ten-foot blades swirled at a powerful speed. There was
nothing I could do but swallow as I stared at what
probably was going to grind me into a bloody pulp.

When I released the line, my body whipped back around
so that I was facing forward. The glow of the light splayed
across the hull. Hand over hand, I pulled myself up the
line. At the point where the rope went under the hull,
there was no gap between my tether and the hull. I

couldn't get enough strength to pull up any more and get clear of the hull.

With a deep breath, I gripped the rope with one hand, feeling the fibers burn across my palm. My feet pressed against the bottom of the ship, and I dragged myself an inch closer, giving me enough slack to unclip the carabiner connecting me to the line. I inhaled a lungful of air, praying it wasn't the last I ever took, let go of the line as I kicked off the hull.

My right leg kicked in quick motions as I stroked down away from the ship. The drag pulled at me, and I continued kicking down. The glow of the flashlight beam waved around as my only thought was to get away from the ship.

Don't look back.

I felt the water pressure against my eustachian tubes in my ears, but I ignored it. Busted ear drums were the least of my concerns at this second. My breathing increased, and my legs, particularly my right one, burned from the exertion.

The water behind me boiled and churned, sending me into an uncontrollable swirl that rolled me end over end. In that instant, I knew I'd lost the battle. My eyes squeezed shut as I tumbled toward the propeller.

Then I righted myself as the whipping about turned into a slower roll. Water pushed me back, and I bobbed up to the surface. The lights of the freighter headed north across the black sea. I lifted my wrist, shining the light at the stern.

My stomach heaved, sending vomit and bile spewing from my mouth. The regulator spat into the water, and I reached back to inflate the BCD after I finished throwing up.

The wake from the ship pushed me off to the port and concussive waves lifted me up and down on the surface. My head leaned back as I took in the stars above me. My chest heaved as I sucked in the fresh air and watched the ship sail away.

I reached back and checked my air. It was at about 700 psi. When I'd boarded the boat, I'd looked at the gauge and it read close to 1500 psi. I'd sucked down half of it, fighting for my life.

It wasn't enough to get back to shore even if I had the scooter. When I turned toward the lights of Progreso, they appeared a long way off. I guessed I was four to five miles from shore. I rolled onto my back and put my ankles together to kick both feet at the same time. The one fin would push me, and the other foot wouldn't throw off the motion by staying in sync with the right one.

Before I started swimming, I stopped. A whine of an outboard buzzed over the water, and I turned to search for the boat. I spotted the red and green navigation lights in the distance. My flashlight came up as I waved the beam of light at the vessel. It wasn't far off—maybe half a mile.

I used the one fin to kick down and push me out of the water as I shined the light at the boat. It seemed to turn my direction, and I waved both arms above my head, hoping they'd see the movement.

The murmur of the engine grew louder, and the red and green light on the bow came closer. It looked like an inflatable dinghy, and whatever it was, I gasped with relief. A four-mile swim in the dark didn't sound great.

A beam of white light passed over me, illuminating the water around me and blinding me.

"Hello!" I shouted at the occupants.

The outboard slowed as the boat came closer. I only saw the bright light they trained on me. As the engine shifted to idle, the RIB coasted closer.

"I'm glad to see you!" I called out.

The boat came up alongside and the light moved out of my eyes. I blinked away the spots until my night vision returned. Two men leaned over the edge of the dinghy, extending their arms out to me. I grabbed both proffered limbs as the men heaved me on board.

I rolled into the bottom of the boat with my BCD rolling me onto my back like a turtle. I released the buckle at my waist and sat up, pulling my arms out of the vest.

As I sat up, I looked at the four men in the boat with me. None were Latino, as I would have expected. Instead, I stared at four white guys. Two of which held nine-millimeter guns on me. No one said a word.

Shit.

I turned to study all four faces, searching for someone I recognized. As I rotated my head around, something stabbed me in the shoulder. I jerked around to see one man pulling a hypodermic needle away just as everything faded out.

26

Handcuffs pinned my wrists behind my back, and duct
tape bound my ankles. I was lying in the corner of a small
cell. I think it was a cell. My eyes blinked a few times as
I tried to absorb my surroundings. It was a brig. I'd seen
plenty of brigs on board Navy vessels in my time in the
Corps. The only one I'd ever been in as a guest had been
last year when the Navy picked me up off the coast of
Cuba.

I squirmed around until I was face down on the floor
and my butt was up in the air. Like an inchworm, I scooted
forward onto my elbows and used the wall to push myself
into a seated position.

My face was numb from being pressed against the steel
floor. The cell vibrated from the engines with a low,
rhythmic hum. I scanned the brig, noting that outside the
cell there was no one standing guard.

The puncture wound in my neck itched. I leaned my
head over to rub my chin as close to the spot as I could. It
seemed to be a pointless endeavor, and after half a minute,
I gave up.

If I was on a military vessel, there should be a guard nearby. Not having one on guard duty meant little. They could have been called away or reassigned. If they thought I was going to be out for a bit, they might have thought I didn't need supervision.

Again, I let my eyes sweep over the area. Something about the rumble of the deck was different. I couldn't put my finger on what was different. One night, as I was crossing the Caribbean Sea, I heard an unusual rattle on *Carina*. It took some time to isolate the cause, but I found a pulley that was about to fail. Ships and boats always make noise, but they all have a different cadence. Something about this boat sounded different.

The bracelets on the handcuffs were tight around my wrist, and every movement I made rubbed my skin against the metal. I was still wearing the coveralls I'd borrowed on the ship. They were still damp, and I was sweating underneath them.

"Hello!" I shouted.

Who the hell had me? The men in the boat were all Caucasian. As close as we were to the Mexican coast, I would have expected the only military to be the Mexican Navy. Those men weren't even American military.

Were they part of all this? How did they find me?

The obvious answer was that the men on the freighter alerted someone that I went overboard. What is the point of coming for me? They'd have to assume I'd be stranded out there if I'd even survived the fall.

No one came after I called again. My voice just echoed off the walls.

My head dropped back against the wall, and I thought about my predicament. No one knew where I was. Smith would assume I was still on the ship or somehow I'd gotten lost at sea. If they let the ship get all the way to Gulfport before detonating the missiles, it would cause massive loss of life. I didn't want to think about the crew if the ship mushroomed at sea, but at least the crew would be all that died. That was all just my speculation. The other twenty-five missiles might be anywhere.

I straightened up.

Idiot.

Of course, the missiles are here. They offloaded them onto this vessel.

I strained my neck to peer out the bars. They dragged me along with them.

Wait, why do that?

It made more sense to leave me in the ocean. They wanted something more from me. Perhaps they think I know more, or somehow, I'm involved.

After half an hour, it occurred to me I needed to pee. While there was a steel commode in the cell's corner, there was no way for me to use it in my current situation. At least not one that I would register as a success.

It reminded me of a day in early 2005. Stationed on a hilltop with Jay Delp. I was operating as his spotter, and Jay watched through the scope at a camp a mile down in the valley. The challenge to working in the desert was finding the balance of water intake. We'd sweat through three gallons of water a day on average, but when we were in the hills, remaining almost motionless for days, that became a struggle. Most of the water came out in sweat, and peeing became secondary. Of course, when it happened, it was brutal.

On day three, I recall the urge hitting me. I needed to relieve myself, but there'd been too many patrols in the hills to risk unwarranted movement.

"Just do it," Jay whispered. His southern Mississippi drawl often had a way of tricking a person into trusting him.

"I'm not pissing myself," I told him.

"It's only going to get worse," Jay quipped without letting the decibel of his voice rise louder than the wind.

"I'll be soaking in urine for days," I complained.

He made an almost imperceptible shrug. "So be it, but now it's all you're going to be thinking about."

As much as I hated to admit it, he was correct. The pressure in my bladder increased, and I started cutting back on the water I was consuming.

"You still have to drink, Flash," he reminded me.

"It's a never-ending process."

"Welcome to the sniper nest," he joked. "Guess you won't volunteer again, huh?"

"No one else wants to spend a week in a hole with you."

Jay didn't move as he fell silent.

Two hours later, I'd grown restless. The urge to pee was all I thought about. It drove me to want to squirm.

"Just fucking go," he groaned.

I lay there for another ten minutes before I relented. As soon as I did so, I heard the soft chuckle from Jay.

"You pissed your pants, didn't ya?" Jay mumbled.

"Yeah," I replied.

His head bobbed as he laughed. "I can't believe you did it," he joked.

"You said to."

Jay continued to laugh. "Yeah, but you did. Fucking Marine that pisses his pants. I can't believe it."

"Shut up, Jay."

It wasn't until we got back to camp that I saw him remove a pair of adult diapers. When he saw me notice, he burst out laughing again. Turned out he'd planned it from the start.

In the brig now, I laughed to myself. The memory was one of our first times in the field, and it was the start of a lifelong friendship.

But it only worked as a reminder that I still had to pee, and while I might ruin a pair of fatigues in the field with Jay, I'd be damned if these guys came in to find me in a puddle of my own urine. I'd hold it.

An hour passed before I heard the clunk of a door outside the cell open.

"Hey!" I shouted.

A gruff face appeared in the small opening. "You're awake," a voice remarked, and I recognized the man as one from the tender who fished me out of the ocean.

"Yeah, I need to take a piss."

He nodded. "You're wanted on the bridge," he told me.

"Not without some help," I explained. "And not before I drain the oil."

He grunted and studied me. I hadn't moved from the corner. My arms were aching from the position behind my back, and I wanted to stretch a bit. However, I suspected they had left me like this intentionally. It would make it difficult to fight or flee if my limbs were numb and stiff from being stuck in the same position.

"Come on," I begged. "I need to go."

The brig door open inward, and the man stepped inside. I hadn't gotten a good look at him last night. The bright spotlight and sudden darkness played havoc with my sight, and by the time I regained my vision, they had drugged me.

He was tall and muscular, and the tight black t-shirt clung to his torso. I saw the abs on the guy, and he reminded me of a gym rat.

He stepped up to me, looming over me. His thick hands grabbed me by the coveralls and jerked me to my feet. He dragged me across the cell. My bound feet trailed along across the floor. At the commode, he lifted me up enough to let my feet settle on the deck.

"Why don't you take these cuffs off me so I can do my business?" I suggested.

Instead, the man unzipped the front of the coveralls, running the zipper to the middle of my thigh. He yanked the shoulders down, stripping me from the neck to my waist. My cuffed hands stopped the sleeves from coming off and left me bound tighter than I had been with just the shackles.

"Come on, dude," I moaned. "Have some decency."

Gym Rat lacked any such thing, and he didn't allow me any as he reached around and dropped my swimsuit down.

"Seriously?" I snapped.

"I'm not going to aim it for you," he grunted.

With a sigh, I relieved myself. After a minute, I finished.
"I don't suppose you could give it a shake for me?" I
asked with a satisfied smugness.

"Cute," he remarked.

"No one's ever called it cute," I considered. "Your
girlfriend just called it better."

He ignored my quip. Girlfriend jokes didn't get under
his skin. Maybe I should have insulted his mother.

Gym Rat pulled my shorts up in a swift motion, giving
me a wedgie unlike any I'd had since junior high. He pulled
me back from the toilet, still holding the bunched-up
coveralls binding my upper arms.

"Thanks," I told him. It wasn't the smartest course
of action to insult the guy who just helped you pee.
Sometimes my snark or fight mode was difficult to turn
off.

"Move," he ordered, without acknowledging my
gratitude.

"Can you at least cut the tape on my feet?" I asked. "It
will be easier than having you drag me everywhere."

Gym Rat considered that for a second. He pulled a
stiletto from his back pocket. The snap of the blade
springing out from its handle echoed against the metal
walls. He knelt over and cut through the duct tape in a
single motion. It was a sharp blade.

I took a second to rotate my ankles around, stretching
the muscles that hadn't moved in hours.

"Let's go," he ordered.

Without hesitation, I let him push me through the brig
door. This wasn't the time to start a fight. Not only was

any movement in my upper body hampered, it wasn't the time. I still didn't know where we were or what was going on. Without a little more knowledge, I might find myself in a worse situation.

When we exited the detention area, I paused at a set of narrow steps.

"We're on a sub," I remarked.

"Yeah," Gym Rat admitted. "Get up the steps."

I stared at him a second before letting my eyes trail up the steep stairs.

As if he read my mind, he remarked, "I'll be behind you."

His reassurance alleviated little in my mind, but whatever they had in mind didn't involve me being dead. For the moment, I had to trust that fact.

My ascent was slow as I took each step with my left shoulder pressed against the bulkhead as if it were a handrail. It was known that in the Navy, a lot of purple hearts came from falling on a ship, making that one of the leading causes of causalities in war.

The next level was busy with six men moving around manning the stations. I'd only been on a couple of submarines during my service, and I spent those times in a cabin only. In fact, the only time I'd been in the operational center of a submarine was an old German sub I found in the Bahamas at the bottom of the sea. That one hadn't been operational in over eighty years.

The bulkhead had painted instructions, most in Spanish or Russian. I guessed this was an old, decommissioned model from Cuba's navy.

"Keep going," Gym Rat urged as I trudged through the area. I noticed the guy at the radar station studying the blips on his screen. He was tracking a ship, but there were no designations on the monitor to identify it. Obviously, he knew what it was he was watching.

"Up!" Gym Rat ordered when I reached a ladder leading to the next deck.

"My hands?" I asked.

"I'll be behind you," he repeated. This time I found the thought less comforting.

"You expect me to climb a ladder without my hands?" I questioned in a loud voice to be heard over the din of the sub.

"Or I can drag you up by your hair," he retorted. His eyes narrowed to two black beads. Perhaps he was taking revenge on the girlfriend quip earlier.

My head turned up to follow the rungs of the ladder. There were only six of them before they vanished above to the next deck. I figured once I cleared the hole, I could use my back against the edge of the opening to stabilize the rest of my climb. None of it was ideal, but I got the feeling Gym Rat would have no qualms about dragging me up by my hair.

"But you got my back?" I asked.

The goon grunted, and I sighed. When he placed his hand against my back, I picked up my left foot and placed it on the first bar. A second later I was three rungs up and Gym Rat still kept his hand pressing me against the ladder.

My head prairie-dogged up through the opening, and I attempted to take in what I saw while maintaining an awkward balance on the ladder. My lower back cleared the ledge, and I leaned back against it as I pushed my ass over the lip with my legs. Once I was through the opening and lying on the deck, I rolled over to my knees. My eyes darted around the room, looking for an escape.

Although, where could I go? If we were on a submarine, we could be a thousand feet down. I'm not sure what the world record for unassisted ascent was, but I didn't have a great desire to attempt that.

The predicament I was in dawned on me. I was stuck for the ride. The only way off the vessel was if it was at the surface. If I got free and sabotaged it, then I'd still be at the bottom of the sea.

That wasn't a prospect I wanted to choose.

"Is this Mr. Gordon?" a woman's voice asked.

My head rolled over, and I sat up to stare at a young woman with long red hair. I recognized her as the woman who escorted Dani from the restaurant. She wore a tan pantsuit that seemed out of place on a sub.

"Yes, it is," Gym Rat admitted as he ascended the ladder.

"Mr. Gordon, so nice to finally meet you," she remarked, bending down to stare at me. Her accent was an odd mixture of Australian and German. Or perhaps it was something altogether different. "You've been quite a thorn in our side."

Gym Rat grabbed me by the bunched-up coveralls at my back and pulled me to my feet.

"Glad I could help," I told her.

She smiled a broad grin with perfect white teeth. "Oh, don't worry, we aren't done with you yet."

27

I stared at the woman with piqued curiosity. "I'm not all that interested in participating," I told her.

She laughed a lilted, infectious laugh that had we been enjoying a coffee in a bistro somewhere, would have intrigued me. However, on the bridge of a submarine hundreds of feet below the surface, the laugh felt like a disease.

"It won't be up to you, I'm afraid."

My mind started turning things over. The question I'd had since I woke up in the brig was, "Why?" So I asked it.

She turned away from me to stare at another radar screen, probably simulcast from the station on the lower deck. "You were only supposed to be a witness," she commented. "Someone to pinpoint Traylor's death."

"Makes sense," I admitted. "If he'd just vanished at sea, there'd be questions. But that only matters if you needed him to be proven to be dead. Why do you need that?"

She turned to look over her shoulder. "Oh, I didn't. Not really," she told me. "But if I was going to stir the pot, then I might as well make something out of the mess."

"Why did you bother killing him?" I asked. "He already made the missiles for you."

She smiled. "Yes, and no. We worked through Carlee to have the missiles made."

"Carlee?" I questioned.

"Needless to say, she had few good feelings toward her father," she explained. "I'm sure Danielle gave you some of those gory details."

It was the way she used Dani's name that felt like a punch to my gut.

"Was Dani in on it?" I wondered aloud.

The woman laughed again. This time it had a near maniacal ring to it. I realized that in a different situation, it would have only sounded amusing.

"No. No, not at all," she denied. "Not of her own volition at least."

"Who are you?" I asked.

"I'm inconsequential," she replied. An obvious lie, even if it was only to me. She believed she was of the utmost importance.

"Then what is all this?" I asked, waving my hands around the bridge.

"This is the ultimate achievement," she grinned, waving her hands around like a game show host. "The peak of my life's work."

"Your life's work?" I repeated. "What are you like, thirty-three?"

"Thirty-two," she corrected. "And I'll do in my brief life what no one has accomplished."

"Which is?" I prodded her.

"Bring about destroying the American war machine with its own weapons."

I gave the inside of the submarine a slow scan that could have doubled as an eye roll. "This is a fifty-year-old Cuban submarine," I pointed out. "It was probably used when the Cubans got hold of it. I don't think it's American made."

Irritated, she snapped, "That's not the point. Traylor's Spike Missiles are made, not only by an American company but one owned by one of the president's largest donors and friends. It will play out in media for weeks, maybe months."

"What will?" I asked.

"The attack," she explained. "A simultaneous assault on America."

"Of course," I remarked. "You deploy the Spikes, where? To cities across the nation? Are you targeting landmarks or government buildings?"

"All of it," she replied. "Twenty-five missiles will launch in just a few days. Timed down to the minute. It will make 9/11 seem like child's play."

"Child's play?" I scoffed at her arrogance. "What do you think is going to happen after you murder hundreds of thousands of innocent people?"

"When it's discovered that the weapons are all American made, the citizens will rise."

I cocked my head at her. "You're kidding, right?"

"Not at all. Within seconds of the attack, the media will get a message from the leader of this attack claiming responsibility."

"Yeah, yeah, yeah," I replied, annoyed. "You remember what happened with 9/11. I mean, you were only a kid at that point, but Al-Qaeda thought they'd bring us to our knees with a coordinated attack. That ended up turning into a twenty-year war."

"It spawned more groups ready to fight the US," she pointed out.

"None of which have done anything significant," I reminded her.

"This will divide the country to a point it cannot recover from," she explained.

I shook my head. "Who is behind this?" I asked.

"We are Demand Peace United."

"Demand Peace United?"

Her face lighted up as she detailed this organization. "We are a group of believers who want to see the world disarmed."

This time, I rolled my eyes. "Disarm the world? I love how you want to do that with arms."

"It's the irony of the event," she explained. Her frustration was bubbling to the top.

I paused and studied the surrounding men. Most of the crew had an air of military training. None of them were pacifists. That was obvious in the few encounters I'd had with them so far.

"Who bankrolls your little peace-loving party?" I asked her.

"It's funded by like-minded people."

My eyebrows raised. "I haven't shopped for a submarine lately, but even fifty-year-old models like this one run hundreds of thousands, if not millions, of dollars. Hell, thirty nuclear missiles cost at least a billion dollars."

She stared at me with vexed incredulity. "People have grown tired with the warmongering government," she stated.

"Not so much that they are dropping a billion dollars. Besides, how does a "Give peace a chance" hippie in what I bet is a three-hundred-dollar suit know about getting a submarine?"

She scoffed at me.

"Who is backing this?"

"We have a consortium who put this together," she explained.

That answer hung in the air. Again, I took a long look at the crew. After my eyes flitted to each one, I asked, "Did they hire your men?"

"They are all part of the organization," she answered.

It morphed from a group of donors to a consortium to an organization. She hadn't realized that all she was in this plan was a minor cog. In fact, I was betting the men behind her selected her as a scapegoat for the entire affair.

For what purpose?

"This organization?" I asked. "How did you get involved?"

She shook her head. "I'm done answering your questions."

"Then why traipse me up here?" I wondered. "Just to gloat that you got me?"

Her head rotated back to stare at me. "No, I have plans for you."

"I assumed as much," I remarked. "Otherwise you'd have left me in the water."

Her smile returned. "That was such good fortune. When I heard you killed our team at the plant and made it to the boat, I knew you were perfect."

"See, I figured I'd just poked at you long enough for you to do something."

"Where is the *Álmodozó*?" she asked.

I recognized the name as the one I'd read on the side of the freighter.

The man she'd asked responded with a string of numbers, "24.954663, -90.033044." He finished by stabbing the middle of the Gulf of Mexico with his index finger.

"How deep is it there?"

"About ten thousand feet."

"Good," she acknowledged with some glee in her voice. "Activate the Spikes."

"Wait," I shouted. "There are people on that boat."

"Sacrificial," she remarked in a cold voice.

I felt the blood rush to my head. Was she so maniacal that she didn't understand what she fought for? Or was it all lip service?

"You're just as bad as these warmongers you rage against," I blurted out.

"No, I don't want to kill these people," she explained. Her voice softened, as if she was assuring me.

"Here's the thing about killing," I stated. "If you don't have to do it, then don't. What purpose does blowing up that boat do?"

"At first, it was to go down without much notice. An unusual blip on a military scope. Someone might search for it, but it would be months or years before anyone got close to finding it."

"Just to hide that you have the missiles?"

"And we want to make sure they work," the woman explained.

"The crew is innocent," I pleaded.

"Everyone is innocent," she told me. "That's the point. It doesn't matter if they are soldiers or shopkeepers. War kills all."

"It doesn't matter," I told her. "By the time anyone knows about the missiles, they won't be able to track them. The three card Monty you played in Progreso assured no one could follow them. Hell, a sub is brilliant. You can sail right up Tampa Bay and offload three crates, with no one ever knowing you were there."

"Precisely," she affirmed. Her countenance beamed with pride. She enjoyed having her plan praised.

"Then don't blow the ship."

"Now, it's even more of a necessity."

My forehead wrinkled. "Why?"

"Mr. Gordon, you were good enough to make an appearance on the vessel," she explained. "Show him."

A monitor on one side of the bridge came to life as a security camera footage played on the screen. A clear image showed me walking through the engine room in my borrowed coveralls.

"You'd been nothing but an annoyance until then," she said. "But now, you became crucial to the plan."

The monitor continued to show me as I made my way to container seventy-two and entered it. While it didn't show me inside the box, the point was obvious that I'd entered it. The footage of the shootout with the crew members seemed to be cut from the footage as well. The last bit showed me going over the railing.

"I get it," I noted with some realization. "You want to make me the villain."

"But aren't you?" the woman asked. "A former American warrior who killed employees at a weapons manufacturing facility and stole nuclear missiles allocated for the US military."

"The military did not order those missiles."

She laughed. This time the mirth was a blatant accusation of my stupidity. "The American government will be covering its ass so quickly that they'll allow a former Marine to be thrown under the bus. After all, they can't let the media find out their systems have been infiltrated. They'll classify it as a theft by a homegrown terrorist. Don't worry, we have a few days to color in the areas of your life that are needed to complete the transformation."

I shook my head. "Then you arrange for someone to gun me down? Wrap it all up in a bow."

"Something like that." Still, she beamed with pride.

"You think you can pass me off as a terrorist?"

"Oh, I can pass off Mother Teresa as a terrorist," she explained.

"Too many people wouldn't buy it," I countered.

She shrugged. "'He was such a nice guy,' 'We never saw that side of him,' or 'He was always such a patriot.'" Her smile stretched wider. "It doesn't matter what the truth is. I only have to handle public opinion."

She wasn't wrong. The news was rife with stories of people who went on killing sprees whose friends and family never saw that side of them. Or ignored it. Would it be so hard to convince the world I was a traitor? Sure, people like Jay Delp or Missy would never believe the stories. But would that matter?

The answer was no. If this woman convinced the media, then they'd have their fall guy. If I died in the process, there would never be a trial for me to claim my innocence. Found guilty by reason of death.

The rage boiled up inside me, and I lunged for the woman. My shoulder slammed into her, shoving her against the radar screen. My head slung forward and smashed into the woman's face, spewing blood from her nose as I broke the cartilage.

Gym Rat jerked me off my feet, and I hung in the air for what felt like an eternity before my back slammed into the metal deck with a clang.

"Lana, are you all right?" someone asked.

"I'm fine," Lana answered with a muffled voice caused by the busted nose.

"Are the Spikes armed?" she asked, and I struggled to no avail under Gym Rat's knee.

"Yes," came an answer.

"Let's see the feed," she requested. At the click of a mouse, the monitor broke up into sixteen squares with images from inside the freighter. I could see the lower hold where I'd found the Spikes, along with the top deck, engine room, bridge, and various other angles of places I hadn't found on the vessel. Several men moved around on the screen as they chugged north through the Gulf of Mexico.

"Now," Lana ordered.

I couldn't see who triggered the missiles, but there was a white flash that seemed to start in the lower hold. In all, it took a microsecond for the screens to all go white as the *Álmodozó* exploded somewhere on the ocean.

28

At least Gym Rat unshackled the cuffs when he threw
me back into the brig. It gave me the dignity to hold
the toilet seat when I vomited. I hadn't considered how
grateful I'd be to do that.

Now I sat on the floor, slowly banging the back
of my skull against the bulkhead. I had realized that
they intended to blow up the ship while I was on it,
but somehow watching it happen on screen turned my
stomach.

That's a good thing, Chase.

I'd seen people die on screen before. I'd killed people
before. But those were all enemies on a field of battle. They
weren't just going about their daily routine.

Even the Traylors who went up on their yacht seemed
different. Until I met Lana, I'd at least assumed Carlee
didn't deserve it. If Lana was telling the truth, she was
behind it.

But not Dani? It seemed from what Lana said, Dani
wasn't involved. Maybe her work with Care for Peace put
her in Lana's orbit. It wasn't a stretch to imagine some
hardliners with the legitimate organization crossed over to

the terrorist arm. Hell, the funding might have come from the same people.

That bothered me, though. The money.

Lana's undertaking wasn't cheap. She had a small army, and none of the ones I'd seen struck me as the volunteer type. Almost all had a mercenary quality to them. How did Demand Peace United pay them?

It was more than just that, though. The plan was chaotic and ineffectual at its core. There was no way a coordinated assault on American soil would disillusion the citizens. It would likely have the opposite effect. The fall of the Twin Towers showed that. Never had the United States been more unified than following that attack. Lana intended to inflict that same damage twenty-five-fold.

I shivered at the thought.

After an attack like that, the country would go into utter disarray. Markets would crash. It would make the economic collapse around 2020 seem like nothing. At least for a few weeks.

But she was right about one thing. The media would need a guilty party. Once Lana delivered one—me, I supposed—Demand Peace United or even Care for Peace could stomp in to champion the cause of disarmament.

It wouldn't go far. War was a billion-dollar affair, and the market wouldn't eliminate it. However, the powers that be would put on a show, add some regulations and audits. All of which would cost money that would come from the taxpayer and line the pockets of people like the Traylors and the politicians they supported.

The only thing Lana was going to do, besides kill hundreds of thousands of people, would be to hasten an economic depression and resulting inflation.

Not to mention, kill me in the process. While in the entire scheme of things, I didn't count. That didn't make me like the situation any more.

I needed to get out of here. Not just that. This submarine had to go down. It was the only option I saw. If we made it to whatever port Lana chose, she could offload the missiles at night and no one would notice. At that point, it was too late.

No, I needed to get out of this cage and sink the sub. At least then, no one else would die.

I pushed myself to my feet and paced around the cell. There was no way out of here, and until Gym Rat returned, I was stuck.

My face pressed against the bars of the door, studying the corridor leading out. The door leading out of the detention area remained sealed. What I wouldn't give for some C-4 right about now.

I wasn't familiar with submarines, but I knew boats. Life on the sea taught me a couple of important rules. Number one was "Keep the water outside the boat." That's followed by "Keep yourself in the boat." If a sailor can follow those two rules, they can almost always walk off onto the dock.

While I didn't know the layout or design of this submarine, I understood the flow of water. It's going to fill in the space and take the path of least resistance.

Of course, the designers of any boat took into consideration rule number one. Because inevitably something broke. A helmsman would run into a submerged pylon or container that fell off a freighter. The latter was a growing fear in the cruising community.

If a hull breach occurred, doors like the one leading out from the detention area could slow or stop the progress of water. That meant I needed to get as low in the vessel as possible. If I could find a seacock or hatch to blow open, the compartment would fill.

This was an old military submarine, and from what I saw on the bridge, it appeared to sport updated equipment. It wouldn't take long for the bridge to know that there was a hull breach. At that point, the crew would go into action to isolate the water. I wasn't sure how much water it would take to sink the vessel.

In *Carina* I had bilge pumps with float valves that kicked on if the water rose too high. I needed to overpower the pumps on the sub. Or disable them.

That plan cemented in my mind. Get down to the engine room and disable the pumps before opening up the seacocks. All while likely fighting off a crew that wanted to stop me from breaking rule number one.

My forehead pressed against the bars. None of that could happen if I didn't get out of this cell.

Frustrated, I pushed off the door and settled on the floor. I didn't mind the idea of dying. It was settling over me, too. There was no way to get out of this alive. At least not if I wanted to keep the missiles from leaving the sub.

Once they hit shore, Lana and her people would divide them up to head for their targets.

It would be a nightmare to stop it after that. Twenty-five nuclear explosions, even small ones, across the country would devastate America. I didn't know what targets she chose, but they'd be large enough to leave a mark. She wanted to injure the country.

While her actions were contrary to her professed beliefs, the core of both Demand Peace United and Care for Peace was ending all war. But disarming the US without doing so to Russia, China, North Korea, or many military states left us defenseless. I didn't think a strike as efficient and deadly as she intended would render America weak. Economically perhaps. Hell, the stock market would crash, and we'd face a depression.

In the hours after 9/11, the markets crashed under the barrage of brokers selling shares. A few people made an absolute fortune out of sheer luck. If one could term anything that day as lucky.

However, if someone realized an event like that was going to happen, they could set themselves up to snag tumbling shares. One could make billions in a matter of minutes.

Of course, they'd have to know when to be ready.

My back hit the wall, and I slid down to the floor. My mind filled with a realization. Lana had support from a consortium. She used that word. "Like-minded people," she called them.

Of course, she wanted to use me as a patsy, but someone beat her to the punch. Lana and the Demand Peace

United—if that was even a real thing—were someone else's puppets. They plucked some idealistic idiot up and set her in motion. If I had the time to search or just talk to Dani, I bet we'd find a connection to Dani's employer, Care for Peace. Lana said Dani wasn't directly involved. Indirectly, though. Perhaps she connected Lana and Carlee without realizing it, even if it were just a matter of saying, "Dani suggested I meet you."

But behind it all, I bet there was a powerful and rich group, or even a single person, prepared to reap the consequences.

I considered trying to convince Lana of the truth. But what did I know? Nothing. Everything was speculation.

The door outside creaked as it opened. Gym Rat pressed his face against the door.

"Lunch," he announced, sliding a sandwich wrapped in a plastic zippered bag through the gap.

My stomach growled, and I realized I hadn't eaten since before Dani and I left Cozumel. Based on my internal clock, that was over twenty-four hours ago now. I pushed myself up and grabbed the sandwich.

"You don't buy into all this, do you?" I asked the guard.

He made a face and rolled his eyes.

"I thought so," I stated. "Can I talk to Lana again?"

"Not yet," he replied.

"At what point do you guys turn on her?" I asked.

He didn't respond, but somehow that was enough of an answer.

I removed the sandwich and took a bite. Bologna and bread. They could have at least added some mayo.

"Is this my last meal?" I asked.

Gym Rat stared at me. "She said to keep you happy for a few days."

The deck shuddered as if the vibrations had slowed a bit.

"How deep are we?" I asked.

His response was a shrug, but I expected little more than that.

"I'd like to have another talk with her," I repeated my request.

"If she wants," he told me as he turned to leave.

I ate the rest of the sandwich. "Next time, can you throw some mustard on it?" I asked.

He turned to glare at me with a furrowed brow.

"Can I get a drink?"

Gym Rat's mouth twisted into a smile and he pointed at the stainless-steel toilet. "There's water there."

I lifted an eyebrow as he vanished through the doors.

He'd said little, but I got plenty from him. I suspected we were nearing our destination. That meant my time was running out. If I was right, Lana's was too.

I just needed to be somewhere other than here when it happened.

29

When I woke up, I figured it was a little over four hours since Gym Rat left me with my bologna sandwich. There wasn't much I could do but pace and worry, so I slept. In the Corps, I learned the value of sleep. Often we'd find ourselves on a mission with no end in sight. Hours of hiking might turn to days or even weeks. And with the enemy constantly on the move, we remained vigilant—a serious detriment to getting rest. I found it important to sleep when I could.

Over time, the body adjusted to what it received. I never suffered from insomnia because, by the time I let my head drop back and closed my eyes, exhaustion overwhelmed me. Twenty minutes here or two hours there would often sustain me for another day.

Once I had a little food, some sleep seemed advisable.

The creaking of the metal door interrupted my sleep. I sat up straight.

The vibrations in the deck had ceased. We were at a full stop. Once I'd realized we were on a submarine, I understood the unusual sensations the ship had been giving off. It had seemed like a distinct language to me

because it was. Once I understood that, I could feel what
she was doing. At least to some extent. Some submariners
who spent years in a tube underwater might pinpoint the
vessel's depth based on the creak in the hull, but I couldn't
do that. Nor did I have a great desire to live on a sub long
enough to learn. I loved the sea, and if I die on it, my
life will seem complete. However, I also like the sun and
horizon, neither of which I can enjoy inside a can under
water.

The door opened, revealing a new person. Maybe
Gym Rat was off duty. Instead, a near identical white
military-type appeared. He had darker hair than Gym Rat,
but otherwise he was a close match. I wondered if I fit into
the same bill. Hopefully, my boat tan, at the very least,
differentiated me from these douchebags.

"Get up!" the douchebag called.

"Where are we?" I asked.

"I didn't ask you to talk," he snapped.

"Ah," I remarked. "Yes, sir."

He was cocky and self-sure. I forced back a smile. Cocky
was a character flaw that I loved to see in an opponent.
Douchebag, here, displayed it in full colors. He considered
himself superior, something I hadn't sensed in Gym Rat.
Neither felt like an obstacle, and if this guy continued the
way he was going, I would get an opening.

He unlocked the door.

"Turn around," he ordered.

I stared at him, letting a faux look of confusion cross
over me. For effect, I added, "What?"

Douchebag stepped into the cell and lifted a pair of handcuffs. "I said, 'Turn around.'"

"He said he wouldn't handcuff me," I lied.

The man crinkled his forehead, expressing his own confusion for a second. "What? Who?"

He stepped toward me as I answered, "The other guy." My tone continued to carry a sense of dismay.

"He's not here," Douchebag explained as he reached for my shoulder to force me around.

As his left arm reached for my right shoulder, I caught him by the wrist, rotating on my right foot to throw him into the bulkhead. Surprised, he let out a barely audible squeak as my left hand caught the back of his head to propel him face-first into the steel wall. There was a crunch as his teeth smashed against the side. His body went limp, and I released him. Douchebag rocked back, landing on his back.

I stared down at his face, now a bloody mess. At least two teeth were missing, and I glanced toward the wall to see where they'd fallen. If he hurried, he might find a dentist who could fix them. Somehow, I doubted that would happen for him.

When I dropped to my knees, I gave him a quick pat-down, retrieving a small hunting knife from his belt. Otherwise, he didn't have another weapon. After slipping the blade into the pocket of my coveralls, I grabbed the handcuffs. They might come in handy.

As I left, I pulled the door closed and removed the keys, still dangling in the lock. Douchebag wouldn't be going anywhere until someone came and rescued him.

When Gym Rat escorted me up the narrow metal stairs, I noticed another ladder toward the aft section of the sub. If I intended on sinking the vessel, I needed to head toward the stern.

Was it still called a stern on a submarine?

Probably, yes. Although I might look that up once I got out of here. I shook my head as I realized I would not get out of here.

When I stared down the ladder, I could see the deck below. Heat came up through the opening, and I wondered if that meant I was close to the engine room. I slid down the ladder, finding myself in a small corridor.

Since I'd only gone up from the brig with Gym Rat to reach the bridge, I guessed I was still mid-ship. I continued down the hall toward a low drone coming from the other side of a hatch.

The metal door swung open into a brightly lit room. Light bulbs in metal cage fixtures popped out from the low-hanging ceiling, and I kept ducking to go under them. There was about an inch of space, but the room felt small. In the middle of the space, a giant diesel engine hummed along. Two men were in the back, leaning over a screen. Both seemed enthralled by what I realized was an iPad.

The small knife came out of my pocket as I approached the men. Neither turned toward me, and I crossed beside the engine in two strides.

The knife in my right hand struck out in a swift, decisive strike that drove the blade into the neck of the man on the right. I let go of the handle as a gurgle escaped his lips. The other man, surprised, jerked around in time for me to drive my left fist into his throat. He reached for his neck, and I jerked the knife out of the first man. The motion caused the blade to slice through the man's neck muscles as it came out. Any life left in him spilled out as he fell to the deck.

I whipped the blade toward the other man, who realized what was coming for him. He dropped toward the deck, rolling under the stainless-steel workbench. I stepped back, pulling the table away from the wall. As the crewman scrambled to his feet, he grabbed a long pry bar used to install the large drive belts on the diesel. The engineer choked up on the bar like a bat and swung it at me. His bar was a yard long, and I hopped back to avoid the end. He shifted on his feet and took another swing at me.

I pulled back, bringing my knife hand over my shoulder. His concentration locked on the blade, and I stepped forward with my left foot, driving my fist into his face. The blow surprised him, causing him to stumble back. The man was deft on his feet though, and he recovered, lifting the bar like a two-handed sword. Rage filled his eyes, and he charged at me, swiping the bar forward with ferocious speed.

This time I stepped back with my left foot, bringing it around behind my right. My body twisted as I followed through the spin. The man was already on his backswing, and when my right foot came around, I lowered my torso to barrel into him with my left shoulder.

Both of us came off our feet and slammed into the diesel engine. An uncovered whirring belt caught the edge of the pry bar, flipping it out of his hand. The bottom of the bar caught me under the chin, and I fell back to the floor.

Seconds passed before my senses returned. I blinked hard, trying to orient myself. The engineer stood against the engine, staring at me. On the deck, I realized I was at his mercy, and I rolled away, crawling to my feet. My head swam, and I tasted blood in my mouth.

The engineer still didn't move, and when I looked into his eyes, I realized he couldn't. The belt had caught the back of his shirt, winding itself into the machinery and tightening around the man's torso. His face developed a shade of blue as his collar strangled him.

I realized I'd dropped the knife when I got knocked down, and I bent to retrieve it. With a swift strike, I sliced the man's neck, speeding along his inevitable demise.

Now, I was alone in the room.

Pumps, Gordon. Turn off the pumps.

I rotated around, looking for any sign of the pumps. There were walls of switches, most of which were in Russian, with a few translated to Spanish. Not that either of those helped me any. The best that I could do was just start flipping switches. How long would it take before the bridge realized something was going on down here?

Fuck it.

I started on the right and began flipping switches. If the light was green, I turned it to red. If it was glowing, I tried to turn it off.

About halfway through the first panel of lights, I heard the shout.

"Stop right there."

I looked over my shoulder to see Gym Rat holding a nine-millimeter Beretta on me.

30

"You get around," he remarked without emotion.

"The guy you sent to take your place was a little sloppy," I pointed out.

"Come on," he ordered. "Leave the knife."

I glanced down at the bloody blade still in my hand. For a split second, I wondered if I could throw it at the goon. The answer to that was a resounding no. Knife throwing was one of the few skills the Marines tried to teach me I never got right. Not never. I hit my target at least three times out of ten. Not great odds, and I wasn't willing to gamble that I could do it now.

Instead, I released the hilt, letting the knife bounce off the deck. I started toward him. Gym Rat stepped back, staying two strides away from me. He was smarter than the douchebag, knowing that all it took was to get inside my radius for me to attack. By staying far enough out, he had plenty of time to react if I lunged at him. The nine-millimeter would drop me before I closed the gap.

"Bridge?" I asked.

"Sure," he replied, somewhat offhandedly.

I climbed the ladder. The task was easier with both hands, and I hoped he didn't decide to cuff me. Since he hadn't so far, I had to assume he didn't have a pair on him. The cuffs I took off Douchebag were still in my pocket, and it didn't seem prudent to point that out to Gym Rat right now.

When I reached the bridge, I saw Lana standing over to one side watching a screen with a video image of the top of the submarine. It was nighttime, and we were at the surface. Two men on a twenty-five-foot fishing skiff were tying up to the sub.

They were offloading the missiles. Nothing I'd done in the engine room would stop it. I was starting too late.

Defeated, I studied the boat on the screen. It was a Boston Whaler center console. The numbers on the front were visible. AL 3468-T.

AL. Alabama.

I saw the faint outline of buildings. We were in Mobile Bay.

Brazen of Lana. There was a naval shipbuilding facility in this bay, and I guessed the Navy had better ears on the bay than the Coast Guard.

"This is getting out of hand, Lana," I said.

She turned to glare at me. She made a strange face.

"What is he doing up here?" she asked.

The hair on the back of my neck straightened.

"Take him back to the brig," she ordered.

A man from behind her stood up, and Lana spun around.

"What is going on here?" she demanded.

The man who approached her was older than Gym Rat.
I saw a tattoo on his arm. He was a Seal.

"You're no longer in command," he informed the
woman.

"What are you talking about?" she asked.

"You've gone as far as we can let you."

Lana rotated around as her eyes widened. "I don't
understand."

"They played you," I told her.

The woman turned to study me. "What did you do?"

I shrugged. "It wasn't me," I explained. "Your backers
just didn't care about your peace project."

"Of course they did," she blubbered, turning to the Seal.

"Sorry, Lana," he replied. "I got my orders."

I scanned the room. Besides Gym Rat, Lana, and the
Seal, there was only one other guy on the bridge. He was
manning the radar, and from the expression he was passing
between Lana and the Seal, he didn't know which side he
landed on. The confusion on his face told me enough. If
I made a move, he would be the last one I needed to deal
with.

"What are you talking about?"

"I'd guess they plan to use your nukes to do what you
planned," I told her. "Only they plan to let you be the
scapegoat."

"Smart guy," the Seal remarked.

I offered him a knowing glance. "That's not a huge
compliment from a Seal," I told him.

He returned my jab with a nonchalant smirk.

"But you're the scapegoat," Lana muttered, pointing at me. "He can be it."

"It doesn't play as well," I suggested. "Sure, I could pass as a homegrown terrorist with the right doctoring to my background. But you'd never get it all. There'd still be questions."

Lana stared at me.

I continued, "But a mindless goon. I'd look even better for that."

"See, you are smart," the Seal replied with a grin.

"Still not a compliment."

"Ellison, you're going to kill me?" Lana questioned the Seal. Desperation dripped from her words.

"It's nothing personal," he told her. "It just solves the problems."

"Not here though," I pointed out.

Ellison gave me a stern glare. "No, not here," he confirmed, adding, "At least, not her."

The threat was apparent. They still needed Lana for a bit, but I offered them nothing useful. In fact, Ellison had enough experience to know that the longer I stayed alive, the more trouble I could cause.

Fear washed over Lana as she realized they intended to kill her. It had taken a full minute for her brain to wrap itself around what was coming. Once it formed, she reacted. Neither man was ready when she bolted forward.

Instinct kicked in to the two men. Ellison was out of reach of Lana, and he blurted out, "Get her!"

Gym Rat obeyed—a mistake. He lunged for her, stepping inside my radius. As soon as he did so, my left elbow broke his nose. The sudden impact echoed between the bulkheads as his head snapped back. After hitting his face, my hand swept down, grabbing his wrist and wrenching the Beretta out of his grip.

"Fuck!" the man shouted as I tossed him to the deck.

Ellison reacted with a Smith & Wesson forty-five from the small of his back. I threw myself against the ladder and dropped eight feet to the deck below as a gunshot exploded above me.

When I slammed into the rungs, I pulled my legs up as I fell. I hit the next level like a ball. All the air rushed out of me when I landed, and it felt like an eternity before I rolled away from the opening. Everything throbbed at once, but I came up with the Beretta, firing a single shot into the opening.

No one came after me, and after a second, I dashed down the corridor.

The angle of the camera on deck pointed forward, and if I could find a way up top, maybe I could stop them before they left with the Spikes. A door swung open ahead of me, and a figure lumbered out. Both of us froze in the narrow passageway, staring at each other. The Beretta barked in my hand, echoing throughout the steel can. As I lowered the weapon, the man slid to the floor.

I started forward when something hit me from behind. I fell forward, landing on the dead man on the floor. The Beretta was no longer in my hand as something pummeled me from behind.

In a desperate move, I threw my right elbow back behind me. I hit something with enough force for the person on my back to pull back a second. Twisting around, I punched up at the form. My left fist struck Gym Rat in the face. The hit wasn't solid enough, and it didn't slow him down as he grabbed at me.

He was astride me, and he laid his left forearm across my right hand and neck, pinning me down. I bucked my hips, twisting about as my left hand, still free, reached for his face. My thumb and forefinger scratched across his cheek until my thumbnail found his eye. I dug into his eye, and the man released his left arm to grab at mine.

Still bucking, I drove my right fist up, hitting him in the jaw. Between my digging at his eye and thrashing, he lost balance. I rocked him to the side, clambering over him. He thrashed at me, hitting me twice.

Now that I was on top, I dug my thumbnail into his eye. Gym Rat howled, and I used the leverage to slam my forehead into his face. I jerked his head up and pounded it down onto the deck. Again and again.

After the third time, I felt the life leave the man. I dropped his head and got to my feet. The Beretta lay next to the man I'd shot. As I stood up, I scooped the gun up and ran through the door.

The next section was a storage compartment, and a ladder led up onto the hull. A cool breeze blew through the hatch into the room. I grabbed the rung and climbed into the night air.

Aft of me, I could see the Boston Whaler bobbing alongside the submarine. The water in the bay was churning with eight-foot waves. Ellison stood on the top

hull, gripping Lana in his arms. The two swayed as the
submarine and the skiff rocked in the furious sea.

They hadn't killed her yet. She was either still valuable
or Ellison planned to dispose of her somewhere.

The Navy Seal turned and saw me. He threw the girl
onto the skiff and raised his gun. The man was still
seventy-five feet from me, but I ducked back below deck
as the bullet whizzed above me.

I counted to ten and popped up, firing toward the
Boston Whaler. Ellison was now on board the boat, and he
returned fire. As I stretched across the hull, I stared down
the barrel and squeezed the trigger. The Seal took cover,
but I was pretty certain my aim was way off.

The Boston Whaler reversed away from the sub, and
Ellison fired again in my direction. His shots were off, and
he was only trying to keep me down. As I climbed to my
feet, I fired again at the boat as they pulled away. I broke
into a sprint aft, firing without aiming as I chased the boat.
After twenty feet, I realized the futility of it. They were
already a hundred yards away and picking up speed.

Ellison stood in the back of the boat as another man
drove them toward the inlet for the Mobile River. The
Navy man seemed to have a smug demeanor in his stance,
but then I might have imagined that.

I stared after the boat, realizing that there were
twenty-five nuclear bombs on it, and it was heading
toward the center of Mobile.

31

Why the hell didn't a submarine have a dinghy?

I stared at the inside of the storeroom when I dropped back down into the vessel. If I didn't find a boat, I needed to at least find a phone. Smith might intercept the boat. We were still near the mouth of Mobile Bay, and from the time I'd been on the bay before, I knew it was a long run from here to the river.

As I ran back along the corridor toward the bridge, I skidded to a stop when a figure stepped out in front of me. I recognized the timid man I'd seen earlier working the radar. The Beretta in my hands snapped up. The skinny tech jumped back.

"Wait!" he shouted. "I'm not armed."

The man glanced behind him, and I saw Gym Rat and the other man I'd shot on the deck where I left them.

"You better make it worth me not shooting you," I told him. "I'm having a very shitty day."

"They just hired me to crew the sub."

Shaking my head, I replied, "You realize what they are doing, don't you?"

He nodded.

I shrugged, turning my head to peer down the barrel.

"I didn't at first!" he exclaimed. "Then it was too late."

"At what point was it too late?"

"Did you see that Ellison guy?" he asked. "He's a killer."

I glanced to the two corpses behind him. "What do you think I'm going to do?"

"I didn't know about the missiles until today," he claimed.

"Can you tell me where they are taking them?"

"He's meeting a van at the dock near the convention center."

"What kind of sub is this?"

"It's an old Soviet attack sub. A Foxtrot," the man explained. "I think they got it from Cuba. The Russians sold it to the Cuban Navy."

"How fast can this thing go?" I asked, ignoring the details.

"On the surface? It maxes out around eighteen knots."

"Even in this weather?" I questioned.

"It's 295 feet long. The ride would be rough, but we can hold that speed."

Mobile Bay often sported calm flat seas or, if the tide and wind worked against the sailor, the conditions looked like they did tonight. It would be a rough ride in the Foxtrot, but in that Boston Whaler, it would be miserable. They'd need to keep it slow enough to handle the peaks and troughs of the waves.

"To the bridge," I demanded. "If you want to survive today, you'll get this bitch moving after them.

"The bay is too shallow," he warned.

"Not in the channel," I corrected him.

He was right. Most of Mobile Bay was only four to six feet deep in low tide. High tide only added a couple of feet, and judging from the waves, we'd already missed high tide. It would only get shallower. But there was a channel cut down the middle of the bay that ran forty to fifty feet deep. It allowed the massive number of shipping vessels entry into the harbor.

I followed the tech up to the bridge. A chunky black man sat at the controls that reminded me of the cockpit of a jumbo jet. Two yokes, identical to what I'd seen on airplanes, extended from the console in front of a screen with what reminded me of a navigation chart on it.

The rotund man saw the other tech before he realized I had a gun on the man.

"Did they tell us where to go?" he asked, as his brain registered the Beretta in my grip. "Oh shit."

"Who else is on board?"

The first tech responded, "I think the two in the walkway were all they left. We were supposed to take the submarine back out to sea before anyone spotted us."

"New plan," I informed him. "Full speed ahead. I want to go straight up the bay."

The second guy spoke up. "It's too shallow."

I repeated what I told the other before we came up on the bridge. "Stay in the channel."

"Who do you think you are?" the man argued.

I leveled the barrel toward him. "You just sent a nut job into my country with enough nuclear power to level

Mobile. You can either help me stop them or I can shoot you and drive this fucking thing myself."

The man stared at me, blinking as he wrapped his head around what I said. After several seconds, he answered, "Full speed ahead. Drew?"

The skinny tech said, "Got it."

The pair began working their station in unison. I'd never seen how a submarine was helmed, but as the two coordinated their moves, it became obvious the task wasn't difficult—assuming one grasped the basics—but it required two people.

"Are we all good?" I asked.

The two men grunted an affirmation, and I relaxed, slipping the Beretta into the pocket of my coveralls.

"I need to call in help," I told them.

"Radio room is forward," Drew told me.

The idea of leaving them alone for a minute didn't sit well with me, but I need to reach out to Smith. If he could coordinate with the local authorities, he might cut them off before they made it to the dock.

"Stay on course," I ordered, praying that they understood the unspoken threat if they disobeyed.

Neither man acknowledged me, and I left them. The radio room wasn't much larger than a broom closet, with panels of lights and knobs. It had been a while since I used a radio to make a phone call, and while it wasn't impossible, the irony of advanced technology made it harder. However, I let out a sigh of relief when I saw a satellite phone next to the VHF receiver. The phone wouldn't work when the submarine submerged, but as long as we chugged along on the surface, I could call out.

"Smith," the agent answered after three rings. He sounded frustrated and out of breath.

"It's Gordon," I told him.

"Gordon!" he shouted. "Where the hell are you? There's been a report of a potential nuclear explosion in the middle of the Gulf. That freighter you were on lost contact."

"They blew it up," I told him.

"With the Spikes?" he questioned. "That wasn't a big enough explosion for all of them."

"It was only five," I explained. "They took the rest off the ship onto a sub."

"Shit, you're on the sub?"

"Yeah, in Mobile Bay."

"Alabama?"

"Yes, listen, Smith," I demanded. "There is a Boston Whaler carrying twenty-five Spikes toward the Mobile River. I think they plan to dock near the convention center."

"And you're on the sub?"

"In hot pursuit," I remarked.

"In a sub?" His tone was doubtful.

"All I had," I told him. "You need to get the cops or the Navy to those docks. If they make land, their plan is to split them all up."

"Who are they?"

"I'm not sure. It was supposed to look like a group called Demand Peace United. They planned an organized attack that would all happen at once."

"I've heard of them," Smith reported. "Extremists."

"Misguided," I added. "But that's all a manipulation by someone else. Whoever put the money behind this effort. The guy with the missiles is a Navy Seal named Ellison."

"Stay on the line," Smith ordered. I heard a click as he put me on hold, hopefully to call in extra support.

The engines churned, and the sub vibrated as it pushed through the wave.

"Gordon?" Smith asked when he came back on the line. Without waiting for me to respond, he continued, "I've got the Mobile Police heading to the convention center. According to the captain I spoke with, there's a dock behind the convention center. It's in the middle of downtown Mobile, right at the mouth of the river."

"Can they get a chopper up in the air?" I asked. "If they get past the cops, someone needs to track them."

"I don't know," he admitted. "I'm working with the Navy too. They might get a helo in the air from Pensacola."

None of it made me feel good. If Ellison spotted the cops on the dock, he could head up the river or just cross to the other side of the river. The Spikes were small enough to move by hand. Once they made it to shore, it would be like finding twenty-five needles in a haystack the size of the continental United States.

"Keep your line open," I told him. "Let's hope we can catch up to them."

I disconnected. Talking to Smith wasn't solving any problems right now. I needed to catch the damned Boston Whaler.

Something dawned on me, and I ran back onto the bridge. Drew and his partner were still manning the helm, and a speed indicator on their screen stated we were traveling at 19.6 knots per hour.

"How long to reach the mouth of the river?" I asked.

"We have to divert around Gaillard Island," Drew explained, pointing at the chart where an island sat in the middle of Mobile Bay. "Based on that, we are twenty miles to the river. But we have traffic in the channel."

"Screw them," I announced. "Is there a way to see Ellison's boat? Does it show up on radar?"

"It's small and in these waves it's hard to locate, but it should be right there." He touched a dot on the radar screen that blinked sporadically as the radar lost and regained contact.

"I don't suppose there are any torpedoes on this thing?" I asked.

Both men turned to look at me with confused, blank stares.

"Do you know?" I asked.

In a synchronized motion, they shook their head.

"You don't know? Or no we don't?"

"There aren't any."

It was a stupid long shot, and even if we did, I'd never fired a torpedo. Somehow I doubted Drew or Chunks had either. Both seemed like they came from the private sector instead of the military. For a second, I wondered if they answered an ad online for "Submarine Drivers."

"Can we go any faster?" I asked.

"We're wide open now," Chunks answered.

"I could plane out the rear planes. We might buy a
quarter of a knot, but we're topping this baby out."

It almost seemed that Drew was enjoying himself, and
I guessed I couldn't blame him. Other than working for
terrorists, operating almost three-hundred feet of steel
under the water would be a blast. Although, I was used
to being on a bridge where I could see where I was going.
These guys operated off radar and charts.

"Do what you can," I urged.

Drew looked up over his shoulder at me. "Hey, man, I
didn't know what these guys were doing."

His words seemed sincere, but then he might realize
he was facing more than just my threats. Once this was
done, Smith would have some questions for these two.
It wouldn't matter how involved they were or what they
knew. He'd drop them in a hole until he milked everything
he thought he could get from them. Unfortunately for
them, I didn't think it would be much.

I only gave him a curt nod.

On the screen, I kept my eye on the dot that Drew told
me represented the Boston Whaler.

"How fast are they going?" I asked.

"Not very," Chunks informed me. "They might be
doing five to ten knots. These seas are something."

He wasn't exaggerating. Even in this vessel, I felt every
motion. As one who spent a great deal of time on the
water, this was nauseating me. If I were on *Carina*, I could
focus on the horizon, inhale some fresh air, and while it
has yet to happen, in a pinch, hurl my lunch over the

side. Now, I didn't have a horizon, fresh air, or a railing to choose from.

But we couldn't slow down. In the last few minutes, we'd gained on the skiff, closing the gap between us. If we maintained our speed, we'd make it to the river mouth in about an hour. Ellison had a fifteen-minute start on us, but they were proceeding slow. The one piece of luck we had was that the weather was on our side today.

I realized that even if I'd found a dinghy, I might not make much better speed than Ellison was now. While the waves shook us like a martini shaker, the massive sub didn't slow for the crests.

It was now just a matter of time and luck.

32

We were now only a mile behind the Boston Whaler, and while we were still doubling their speed, they were entering the mouth of the river now.

"Talk to me, Smith," I demanded when I called him back. "Are the cops in place?"

"Captain Calsac assured me they were getting into position."

I wanted to ask what that meant. How many men did they have? Had they calculated every avenue of escape? Was there a chopper in the air?

All of that went through my head. Any time I lead an operation, I wanted to see all possibilities. Of course, that was never possible. But countless commanders instilled me with a motto of "Failure to plan is planning to fail." It was a creed repeated through most basic trainings, and I expected it was in some military training manual. Maybe someone famous coined the phrase, and we should credit George Washington for it.

Right now, though, I felt like failure was looming over us. I stepped close to the screen and stared at the chart where the mouth of the river opened into the bay. The convention center was about a mile and a half upriver. As long as Ellison didn't see us charging up his six, we might catch them.

The problem was their Boston Whaler offered a great deal more maneuverability in the narrow river than the Foxtrot. At some point, Ellison would realize we were here, if he didn't already. I thought they were too busy keeping their lunch down in the little skiff to notice the lights behind them. Besides, we were still far enough back to only be lights at this point. But once we were close enough, he'd know.

Unless.

"Can we submerge?" I asked.

Chunks turned to stare at me again, a technique he seemed to master.

"Can you?" I repeated.

"Yes," Drew answered. "It's only about forty feet here, though. We need to get all the way to the bottom if we want to avoid any ships on the surface."

"Are there any between us and Ellison?" I asked.

He shook his head.

"Guess it won't matter," I said in a blunt voice. "Go down. If you need to scrape the river bottom, do it. I want to come up underneath that bastard."

Drew nodded and gave Chunks a nod. The other man groaned, but he adjusted a few dials and switches before he pushed the yoke forward. Between the pitch of the boat in the waves and the sudden downward dive, I felt like I might lose my footing. Within seconds, though, we were under, where the waves on the surface didn't toss us about. I let out a breath, grateful for the reprieve from the weather.

The hull popped as we sank down. I watched the blip that was Ellison. He was nearing the docks behind the convention center.

The digital readout of our speed dipped down to sixteen knots as we cut beneath the river. There were a few tankers and towboats pulling barges along the river. Our depth reached thirty-six feet. That reading came from a sonar device, not unlike the one I had on *Carina*. I installed mine in the hull about eighteen inches from the keel. The readings, though, gave me the number of feet from the tip of the keel to the ocean floor. Despite that, I liked to give myself some leeway. In the Foxtrot, I did not know where the sonar was. If I asked that question, it might distract the two helmsmen, so I kept it to myself. And I hoped they knew how close the top of the conning tower was to the surface.

Another tanker blinked on the screen, and I watched it. We were over a hundred yards port of it, but it was big enough to have a draft we might not fit under.

I could feel the hull level out after having made the dive.

"How far off the floor are we?" I asked.

"Right now, eight feet," Drew responded.

"Let's hope we don't snag a tree or anything," Chunks scoffed.

I was growing fonder of Drew than Chunks. "I'm hoping we can stop this terrorist attack you've been a part of," I scolded the man, reminding him of the trouble he was in.

"We're gaining on them," Drew interjected, pointing at the screen where Ellison's red dot slowed to a stop.

"They're trying to dock," I realized. "In this rough water, they'll take it slow."

If they saw the cops waiting for them, though, they might change their plans.

"Shit, I lost them," Drew informed me.

The boat had gotten close enough to the dock to become part of the background.

"When will we be under them?"

"Three minutes," Drew answered.

"Great, I want you to ram this submarine right up Ellison's ass. Come up under them."

"We'll ground," Chunks argued. "Tear through the hull on the pylons."

"I don't care," I stated. "We'll be shallow enough to abandon ship. Hell, if we do this right, you can walk right off onto dry ground."

Drew nodded and gave his partner a stare that told him to just comply.

"I'm going forward. Make sure that when we stop all forward movement, the hatch is near the surface."

"We'll try," Drew said with less confidence than I would hope.

It didn't matter. Like I'd told them, we'd be close enough to abandon ship. I didn't care how the submarine held up. In fact, I'd prefer it to be damaged enough to not be able to move back out to sea. No point in returning it to its current owners.

I checked the Beretta as I hurried forward. Nine rounds,
including one in the chamber. No time to search for more
ammunition. I'd have to make these count.

The deck of the Foxtrot leaned back as we aimed toward
the surface. The hull creaked at first, but that turned into
a groan and then a grind that squealed inside the vessel.
Outside, I heard a crunch of metal and concrete.

I struggled to stay on my feet as the Foxtrot impacted
with the pier, riverbed, and boats on the surface.
Something popped, followed by the sound of spewing
water. We'd breached the hull.

The movement stopped as the submarine settled against
the debris. I grabbed the rungs of the ladder, climbing to
the hatch. It took six twists of the wheel to release the
opening and swing it open. Water poured past me, and I
realized we were still a foot below the surface.

The gush of water knocked me off the ladder, and I
crashed onto the deck below. The muddy river water filled
the compartment and flowed aft through the open door.

If I didn't close that hatch, the river water would
continue to fill the rest of the sub. I needed it to only
fill this storage room—at least enough to stop the rush
through the opening. I'd never be able to get past that flow.

Luckily, the door swung into the compartment I was in,
and I just had to get behind it to swing it closed. Once I'd
moved it ninety degrees, the rushing water flow worked
with me to slam it shut.

The two helmsmen would need to evacuate a different
way. But that wasn't my problem. I stood in the room as
the water reached my waist. As I moved toward the ladder,

I fought the water. Once I got there, I wrapped my arms through the rungs to stay near the opening.

I expected the lights in this section of the sub to go out soon, and it would be more difficult to feel my way out of a pitch-dark cavern. If I was already at the ladder, I only needed to go up.

The water reached my neck, and the smell of it overpowered the rest of the air. It had the stagnant odor of oil, grime, and fish caused when the water pooled in the structures along the shoreline.

I ascended the back of the ladder to keep my head above water for as long as possible. When there were only a few inches, I pressed my face against the metal ceiling, inhaling a deep breath.

Once I couldn't keep my eyes out of the water, I arched my back to inhale the last pocket of air. I took six quick breaths, hoping to fill my blood with oxygen.

Pushing off the ceiling, I sank back to the bottom, keeping the ladder in my right hand. As soon as the last space in the compartment filled, the pressure subsided. I crawled around the ladder and kicked up as my hands followed the rungs. Everything was black except the faintest glow through the opened hatch. As I passed through the hole, it was like coming into the light, even if the only real illumination came from the city lights around the river.

My head burst through the surface to see mayhem. Waves slapped at me as the tide continued out to sea. The bow of the Foxtrot stuck out of the water at a thirty-five-degree angle. We had lifted Ellison's Boston

Whaler in the air at its stern until the bow submerged, allowing the river to capsize the vessel.

I started crawling toward the nose of the submarine that had shoved itself between two concrete pylons.

When I reached that point, I froze for a second, staring at the lifeless corpse of Lana. It floated face down on the surface. From what I could see, it looked like the Boston Whaler came up as the hull of the Foxtrot shoved through to the surface. The impact crushed the transom up against the bottom of the concrete pier, and Lana must have been there when it happened.

There was no sympathy for this woman who instigated this entire affair, intending to kill hundreds of thousands of people. Now her death might still serve the needs of the people behind it. Unless I stopped them.

I climbed across the gap from the sub to the sunken skiff, floating on its side. The positive flotation inside the hull kept it at the surface. I could scale up the center console's side and make the jump to the pier.

A slight relief hit me when I saw a crate still strapped to the deck. There was a space where the other had been, but at least I knew that half the missiles were still here. As I moved past them, I reached down and released the latch on the strap. The pressure from gravity and weight pulled against the loosened fabric, and the crate rolled into the water. They were still retrievable, but it wouldn't be a straightforward thing to do. I hoped it gave Smith enough time to find someone to secure the scene.

Once that was done, I grabbed the stainless-steel frame around the center console awning. When I stood on the side, I could reach the edge of the pier. It required a small jump to push my weight up and roll onto the concrete.

The pier sat behind the convention center, a tan-colored brick structure. I could only see the back and the loading docks under the building. I ran toward the street, a cove blocked by temporary metal barriers. As I sprinted toward the street, I heard the chopper swooping along the river.

A beam of light shone down from the police helicopter. I followed the light to see two men near a UPS delivery van. It took me a second to recognize Ellison, drenched head to toe, either from the boat ride or he ended up pitched into the river when the Boston Whaler overturned.

He drew his forty-five and fired down the street. I dropped to my knees behind a large potted tree. Three police cars blocked off the road, and the Navy Seal fired at them. The chopper directed his light on the van, attempting to blind him. Ellison, however, didn't flinch, raising his left hand to shield his face as he fired at the cops.

He hadn't seen me yet, and if I could get close enough, I could hit him. There was no sign of the other missiles, and I assumed they were already inside the van.

In a swift motion, I jumped to my feet and sprinted toward the front of the van, keeping the police on their backside. It put me in the cops' field of aim, but there wasn't much I could do about that. They'd blocked off the road, pinning Ellison and his men at the end of the cul-de-sac.

By now, the Mobile PD knew they needed more cars, and I expected them soon. The Navy Seal vanished into the van for a second, returning with a rifle. I squinted to recognize the HK416.

Ellison remained covered by the rear of the van, but he opened fire on the police cars. The HK416 fired thirty rounds in a matter of seconds, shattering the police cars' windshields and headlights as the officers took cover. The magazine dropped from HK, and Ellison snapped a fresh one into the rifle before the first stopped bouncing off the ground.

This time he took his time, having pushed the cops back with suppression fire. Now he took his time to aim. A quick burst exploded out of the barrel, and at least two rounds found their target, striking a cop in the neck and head. Ellison squeezed the trigger to lay down cover fire and keep the officers down.

It was a smart technique. Injure a few men while preventing them from getting around to flank him. While the Mobile cops' numbers were small, it would work—until reinforcements arrived.

Ellison rotated the barrel of the HK416, firing a long burst at the helicopter. The spotlight seemed to spark as the bulb erupted in shards of glass. The pilot pulled away as Ellison fired at the retreating aircraft.

I pulled my Beretta up and, staying low to the ground, ran for the front of the van. The driver spotted me. He stepped out the door with a nine-millimeter and fired in my direction. I was far enough away that the man couldn't get a clear shot, but now that the driver spotted me, I'd be a sitting duck for Ellison and his HK.

Sirens sounded, echoing through the buildings. The driver shouted at Ellison, who pointed toward the helicopter circling back around. The chopper hovered behind the line of police cars. Despite the din of the chaos, the ringing of the police cars grew closer. The police behind the barricade had regrouped, and Ellison hadn't fired again in several seconds.

Was he conserving ammo or just waiting for the right time?

The two men and now a third man, who appeared in the van, were arguing. Or making some heated decisions. They had nowhere to go. If I hadn't arrived in the sub destroying their boat, they might have made for the dock. Now, they seemed forced to wait.

I felt some relief. It would take a few minutes and SWAT would show up. If Smith gave as dire a warning as I hoped, they wouldn't waste any time getting a sniper on them. It was just a matter of time.

My nerves tightened back up as Ellison stepped out of the van holding a Spike missile on his shoulder. The other two men were still shouting, no doubt worried that detonating even one of those small nukes here was too close to survive.

I raised the Beretta, firing as I charged toward the man. The bullets pinged off the van but didn't come close to hitting Ellison.

The *foosh* of the rocket echoed between the buildings and across the river as the small tube flew off Ellison's shoulder, soaring in what seemed like slow motion toward the police cars.

33

At some times, the instinct to survive overrides logic. When the Spike launched from Ellison's shoulder, time came to a crawl. I rotated on my left foot to break into a sprint.

In the back of my mind, I understood the futility of the action. When the Spike detonated, a wave of energy would unfurl from the point of impact, absorbing everything within a block of the detonation. In less than a second, I'd melt like one of those wax zoo figures we got as kids under the fire of a blowtorch.

It didn't matter that there was no safe retreat. Even if I somehow escaped the initial melting wave, the ensuing radiation would take me down. That prospect sounded even worse.

So, I ran for the river, fully aware that I'd never make it to the water and that if I did, it would not matter.

Without looking back, I heard the explosion, feeling the concussive wave of heat at almost the same instant. I fell forward into the asphalt, not even bothering to catch myself before my face and chest scraped into the tar.

Another boom followed a second later, echoing from the sides of the buildings and across the river.

Why am I still alive?

I've never been near or even witnessed a nuclear test, but years of training and decades of movies told me I should be dead. Instead, I felt the searing burn from the scrapes on my face.

With almost careful determination, I pushed up to look back. The row of police cars burned like a pyre in the night. The helicopter was gone, but I didn't know if the missile destroyed it, too.

My eyes blinked, trying to catch my brain up to what happened. The UPS van's tires squealed as it barreled past the burning cop cars like a football player through the opposing team's line of defense.

There'd been no detonation. Why? I did not know what the specs on the Spikes were. It didn't seem feasible that the operator could turn off or on the nuclear setting. There'd be too much uncertainty that a regular explosion might set off the nuclear core.

Was it a dud? How lucky would Ellison have been if that were the case?

I jumped to my feet, realizing that Ellison was getting away now. I broke into a run toward the street, letting my eyes follow the van past the burning cars until the smoke and flames obscured them from me.

That wouldn't matter. With the river on one side, Ellison needed to go west. He'd stay off I-10, which was only a couple of blocks from here. That would put him in the tunnel under the Mobile River. Too easy to block him in.

No, he'd want to leave himself a way out.

Right now, Ellison needed two things to get away. First, he needed to get as far from downtown Mobile as possible, and second, he needed another car. The UPS van was a great disguise until it wasn't. By now, the Mobile Police Department would have an APB out on the van, making it the most recognizable car they could be in.

He'd change cars in the next two minutes or the cops would catch him. That bought me a small window of time. I crossed the street toward a vacant building with a ten-foot chain-link barrier surrounding it. My hands reached up, grabbing as high as they could reach and heaving my weight toward the top. When I rolled over the upper bar, I was grateful there was no barbed or razor wire across it.

My feet hit the ground in a sprint down the alley. Broken beer and liquor bottles littered the street where people had taken aim at the dilapidated brick structure. When I reached the other end, I found a large cut in the fence, likely done by denizens of the streets who were using the empty building to sleep. Whoever opened it up peeled the chain-link back, and I didn't slow as I ducked and ran through the hole.

In the middle of the street, I stopped in time to watch the UPS van pass at the next intersection. Heading west like I'd thought.

A horn interrupted my brief rest, and I turned to face a man in his sixties behind the wheel of a blue-gray nineties-model Jeep Cherokee.

"Get out of the street!" he shouted at me.

His reddened face soured, and I motioned at him to roll down his window.

"I don't have time for this shit!" he growled.

"Me either. I need to take your car."

"What the hell?" he demanded, and I lifted the Beretta to him.

The bags under his eyes drooped more, and he cut his gaze to the glove compartment. I prayed he didn't reach for a gun because I had no intention of shooting him, and that might make the exchange awkward.

But he seemed to realize he had lost. Defeat covered his face, and I suspected I'd just made someone else's day worse.

"Your phone too," I demanded as he got out of the vehicle.

The man groaned as he passed an old Nokia phone to me. My eyebrow lifted at the antique. At least it wouldn't require a passcode to operate.

"Sorry," I told him again as I slid behind the wheel. I slipped the shifter into first gear and gunned the engine as he called out some terrible names for my mother. Those didn't bother me much since I agreed with most of it.

I turned at the next intersection onto Dauphin Street and raced along a park. Through the trees in the park, I spotted the UPS van on the next cross street. It was sitting still, and I worried that Ellison had already switched vehicles.

The wheel cut left, and the tires bounced over the curb as I threaded between a park bench and a light pole into the park. The tires dug into the sod as I shifted into third and sped across the park, mowing down bushes.

It was late enough that the park was empty. The few people strolling about broke into a dash, trying to get away from what appeared to be a runaway Jeep.

Ellison was on the street, and in the gaps between the live oaks that lined that side of the street, I watched him lift his HK and fire into a man. His head turned toward the commotion I was causing, and he lifted the gun, firing in my direction.

The Jeep slid left as he started firing. Bullets peppered the ground and side door, but I'd put the line of oaks between me and him. Two men were carrying a crate from the UPS van to a green Ford Explorer.

I turned left again to run through a wooden bench just before I spun the wheel right. As the rear end of the Jeep whirled around, I shifted into second and gunned the engine. My left rear fender careened into a parking meter before the wheels caught traction on the asphalt to shoot me forward. Ahead of me, the Explorer sped away.

The Cherokee dodged the brown van left in the middle of the road. Ellison had only a couple of hundred feet lead on me, and I was gaining.

Red lights illuminated as they braked before turning a sharp left at the next corner. The Ford scraped a Buick parked on the street, stripping the panel and knocking its sideview mirror into the street.

I swung the Jeep to the right, downshifting as I made the curve. By the time I angled toward the middle of the next road, my hands worked the gear shift back up to four.

Headlights shone for a second in my face before veering out of my path, and I crossed into the opposite lane, speeding up. As I neared the Explorer, I nudged the left rear bumper with enough force to send it into a fishtail. As its back end spun away, I rammed it with the front of the Jeep.

The interior exploded as the air bag deployed, knocking me in the face and throwing me back against the seat.

Stay focused, Gordon.

When the Jeep stopped rotating around, I grabbed the door handle and rolled out onto the street. My Beretta came up as I circled behind the Jeep.

The Explorer was facing me now, and the driver moved. I fired the gun twice, putting two rounds into the driver.

The passenger door flew open as I fired where I'd just seen Ellison seated. He scampered out of the truck as I fired another round, shattering his window. He came up with his forty-five firing toward where I'd been, but as soon as I missed the last shot, I dropped behind the other side of the Explorer.

While I was crouched for cover, the rear right door opened, and a dazed man stumbled out of the back seat. He turned to face me, squatting beside the truck's front tire. By the time his brain registered that he'd walked out in front of me, I fired the Beretta, hitting him in the forehead.

He fell to the ground, and I pressed against the rubber, taking in a breath.

As I exhaled, I came up and around the rear door with the barrel of the gun ready. The truck was empty except for a wooden crate in the cargo area. Through the other window, I saw Ellison running past the mangled Cherokee toward the park.

After giving another glance at the wooden crate, I dashed around the back of the Explorer. The Spikes weren't in his hands anymore, but if he got away, we might lose any clues to who was behind it.

I sprinted down the sidewalk. As he reached the corner, he turned and fired at me. Pressed against the side of the building, I'd returned fire. Both of us missed our marks.

In my head, I counted the bullets I had left. I thought it was five, but maybe I'd missed one. For all I knew, he might have an extra magazine or two. When I reached the corner, he had already crossed the street, vanishing into the darkened park.

With the Beretta ready, I charged across the street. Anyone who'd been in the park earlier fled for their lives, and it seemed like I was the only one out here.

It wasn't an extensive park, only occupying about two city blocks. But the city had filled it with rows of live oaks whose yawning limbs shaded any light from the city. Only a few lamp posts offered much illumination, and that only lighted up the concrete sidewalks winding around the park.

The chattering of insects in the trees, coupled with the occasional call of a whip-poor-will in the distance, left me feeling alone in the shadows. An aroma of azaleas hung in the air.

I stalked forward, searching the dark for any movement. The bullet hit me before my brain registered the gunshot. It felt like someone hit me in the back with a baseball bat. Pitching forward, I hit the grass and realized Ellison had shot me. Wounded, I knew I had less than a second to turn back. Ellison had gotten behind me—a potentially fatal mistake on my part.

As I rolled around, a shape charged across the grass toward me. The Beretta was under my left side where I'd dropped it in the fall. My left fingers wrapped around the grip awkwardly as I brought the barrel up under my side. The gun singed me as I squeezed the trigger, continuing to roll away.

In the dark, I watched the shadow stumble. My right side went numb, but I pushed up with my left elbow as I recognized the outline of his forty-five pointing at me.

I pulled the trigger. Again and again. Until the hammer clicked. I blinked, realizing the figure of the Navy Seal was no longer in sight. My elbow seemed to give out, and I collapsed onto my back.

As I stared up through the live oaks at the faint glow of stars, I smelled the earthy notes of grass before I closed my eyes.

34

The yellow glow of fluorescent lights accompanied by the hum of a ballast about to fail woke me. I blinked a few times as I tried to remember where I was. My arm ached with a strange pressure, like someone pressing their finger against the fleshy underside.

As I lifted my head, I recognized the familiar hospital setting. The beep of an EKG monitor became all too apparent. My fingers felt bound, and I realized there was a heart-rate monitor attached to my right index, and an IV catheter punctured through the back of my hand.

Without moving much, I started testing the different areas of my body, probing with my mind to find what and how much damage I sustained.

I could wiggle my toes—a plus right off the bat. My fingers moved, even if they were restrained by monitors and such. My neck moved too.

That was a relief. No obvious paralysis.

That asshole shot me. That much came back to me. In the park.

What happened to Ellison, though? Had I shot him too? Or did he escape?

Then I remembered the missiles. If he escaped, he could have gotten back to his stolen car and retrieved them.

My stomach tightened.

I searched through my head to figure out how long I'd been out. My internal clock was out of commission. The only times that happened was when I'd been unconscious for long periods.

It was daylight now, and I remembered the night sky. That meant it was several hours. From the window, I could see the sun in the western sky, making it late afternoon.

"You're awake?" someone asked.

I turned to see a middle-aged nurse with curly brown hair and thin librarian-style bifocals come into the room. She studied the numbers on all the monitors.

"Have any discomfort?"

"I don't know yet," I admitted.

"That's to be expected. You are on some good painkillers."

"How bad?" I asked, worried.

"You could be worse," she admitted. "But you're also not going to be playing tennis for a bit."

"Great," I replied in a flat tone. "Can I get some water?"

"Let me get the doctor in here, and we can get you something."

She turned to leave me.

"Wait," I rasped, realizing my voice was almost nonexistent. "How long have I been here?"

"You came in yesterday morning. I'll get the doctor." She was gone from the room before I could ask anything else.

It was another twenty minutes before anyone came back. My mouth grew more parched, and I cursed the nurse for not bringing me a drink. Never let it be said that hospitals were there for your comfort.

"Mr. Gordon," a balding man in his early sixties announced as he strolled into the room. "I'm Dr. Strickland. Glad to see you're awake."

I nodded, lacking the energy to talk until I got some water.

Strickland lifted me forward and checked my back before letting me back down easy. I hadn't noticed the raw tenderness of that area until he leaned me back. I winced.

"You're going to feel that for a bit," he assured me.

"Bullet wound?" I asked.

He nodded. "Not your first either, I could tell."

I didn't respond. He pulled out an ophthalmoscope, shining the light into my right eye as he examined my pupils with a low humming, "Mmm."

"What's the prognosis?" I asked as he checked the next one.

"We had to go in and remove the bullet," he explained. "It lodged against the right scapula. We put it back together, and I expect it to heal. We'll need to get in there and so some x-rays to ensure it does so."

"Just one bullet?" I asked.

"You were shot twice, but the other exited out the back. You had some arterial damage, but otherwise you got lucky."

"What about the other guy?" I asked.

Dr. Strickland looked over his glasses at me. "There's a visitor that can cover that for you."

I glanced at the door to see Andrew Smith standing there.

"Can he talk, doctor?" Smith asked.

"Just a minute, detective." Strickland took his time checking my extremities, and I guessed he was doing so on purpose. His demeanor with Smith changed, and I wondered how much Smith had bothered him.

After the man finished his thorough exam, the doctor said, "He is all yours. I'll be back later, Mr. Gordon."

When he left, Smith closed the door.

"Detective?" I asked.

"It makes it a little easier to swallow for them than CIA."

"Where's Dani?" I asked.

Smith smiled. "She's here. But I need to talk to you first."

"What happened to Ellison?" I asked.

"You shot him," Smith explained.

"Is he dead?"

Smith nodded. "Yeah, you dropped him. It looked like he shot you first, though."

"He got behind me," I admitted. "What about the missiles?"

"We recovered ten in the truck and another fourteen in a crate at the bottom of the river. Not to mention an entire submarine. You're going to owe the city of Mobile for the damage to their city pier. I believe the engineers think the damage to the pylons was severe."

"They should realize there are bigger concerns," I remarked. "He fired one of the missiles."

"We know," Smith admitted with little concern.

"I expected to die," I confessed. "There was no nuclear explosion."

"Because none of the Spikes had the nuclear components in them."

"What?" I blurted out in surprise. "You told me they were all armed with them."

"Yes, I did," he replied. "Our people are digging into it now. The records at Traylor Tech indicate they had a nuclear core in them."

"What about the one on the freighter?" I asked.

"We confirmed it was a nuclear explosion."

"Son of a bitch," I growled.

"Yeah, it would seem so. Whoever went through this effort did so to get the nuclear material."

"When did they take them out?" I asked.

"We aren't sure they did," Smith answered.

"They put them in those five on the ship and not the rest. It was all a game of three-card Monty."

"That's about the size of it," Smith admitted. "We are working on tracking down the people behind this, but for the moment, it seems they are in the wind."

"Did you find the two guys on the sub?" I asked.

"Oh, yes, they were not helpful. Lana Delano hired them. She has her own history, and none of it connects to anyone. The group Demand Peace United claims she was never associated with them and anything she did was of her own accord."

"Brilliant. I got shot for nothing."

"I wouldn't say that, Gordon. Even without the nuclear capabilities, those missiles could have been used to cause a lot of deaths. We've searched Ellison's home in Rockport, Illinois. We found some credit card numbers under several names. Those were used to rent a few cars and set up hotels in several cities—DC, New York, Chicago, Nashville, Las Vegas, and San Francisco so far. All within the next week. There might be more out there we haven't found yet. We think they still planned to stage an attack."

"That's something."

"Gordon, need I remind you that this is all hush-hush?"

"Meaning don't talk about it," I acknowledged.

"You understand. Until we finish our investigation, this is top secret."

"But," I interjected, "let me guess. I have the utmost thanks of our government."

"We'll pay your medical bills," he assured me.

"What about that talk back on Isla Mujeres about your paying for my time?"

"You turned me down," Smith reported with a grin.

I lifted an eyebrow.

"I'm kidding, Gordon. Don't worry, we'll take care of you. In fact, with your permission, we'll have your boat delivered here."

"I don't think I'll be sailing soon," I told him. "Can you have it delivered to West Palm Beach?"

"I can handle that," he confirmed. "I'm leaving you my card. If you need anything, just let me know."

"Thanks."

"Once you're better, though, I might have some more work for you."

My head shook. "No, thanks."

He nodded as if he didn't hear me. "I'll be in touch."

As he walked out of the room, Dani appeared in the doorway.

"Hey there," she called out. "How are you feeling?"

"Personally, I'm ready to get out of here."

"I don't think that's a good idea, Chase," she scolded.

"Sorry I left you in Mexico," I told her.

She nodded. "It's okay. But when Smith lost you on the boat, I thought you were dead."

"That wasn't my plan, Dani."

She remained quiet and moved closer to hold my hand.

"Any idea what you are going to do?" I asked her.

"Officially, the word is out about my dad and Carlee. The board has reached out to me, and I've already met with them online. Tomorrow I head to Chicago to talk in person."

"Are you in charge, then?"

"According to my lawyer, yes. There's a lot with probate, but thanks to us—or really you—we avoided a major catastrophe. They don't want that getting out, so I can do just about anything."

"The nukes?" I asked.

"That's number one on the list," she replied. "I have to find that material. There's only the paperwork to say it ever existed."

"Scary," I said. I winced as the muscles in my back ached.

"Are you okay?" she asked.

"Tired, I think."

"I'll get the nurse in here," she replied.

"Wait, you have to go to Chicago, right?"

"Tonight," she answered.

"When can I see you again?"

Dani smiled. "Well, I don't know. I talked to Clayton."

I guess the expression I gave her was pure confusion.

"My fiancee," she clarified.

"Oh, right," I recalled. "Guess I forgot about him."

"Listen, Chase," she started.

I tried to raise a hand. "I get it," I told her.

"It's just if I'm going to change this company, it's going to take a lot of time."

My mouth forced a small grin. "You didn't tell me what Clayton does," I pointed out.

"He's a lawyer."

The forced smile shifted into a forced smirk. "A lawyer is pretty respectable for the head of a big corporation."

"It's not like that," she lied.

"No, I know," I lied back. "But you'll be busy, and I'll be traveling."

Dani reached over and squeezed my hand. "Once I get things settled, though," she remarked.

"Then you'll have Clayton," I reminded her.

Resignation spread across her face. "Yeah, I guess so."

I held her hand, feeling the cool skin for a few seconds. Her touch was gentle, and she reached up to stroke my forehead before leaning closer to kiss me. I don't know how long she sat there, but soon those wonderful drugs kicked in and I dozed off.

When I woke up, I found myself alone in the room with
a single thought
   Who had the nukes?

Also by Douglas Pratt

For a list of books and series by Douglas Pratt
visit www.douglas-pratt.com
or scan the QR code.

9 781960 651051